D1446240

CAST A WIDE LOOP

Cast a Wide Loop

Richard Prosch

THORNDIKE PRESS
A part of Gale, a Cengage Company

GALE
A Cengage Company

Copyright © 2023 by Richard Prosch.
Thorndike Press, a part of Gale, a Cengage Company.

Thorndike Press® Large Print Hardcover Western.
The text of this Large Print edition is unabridged.
Set in 16 pt. Plantin.

LIBRARY OF CONGRESS CIP DATA ON FILE.
CATALOGUING IN PUBLICATION FOR THIS BOOK
IS AVAILABLE FROM THE LIBRARY OF CONGRESS.

ISBN-13: 979-8-88578-943-1 (hardcover alk. paper)

Published in 2023 by arrangement with Richard Prosch.

Printed in Mexico
Print Number: 1   Print Year: 2023

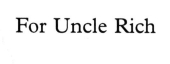

For Uncle Rich

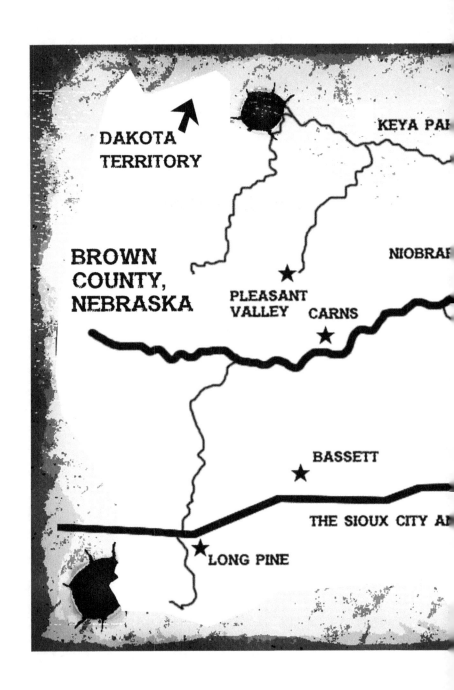

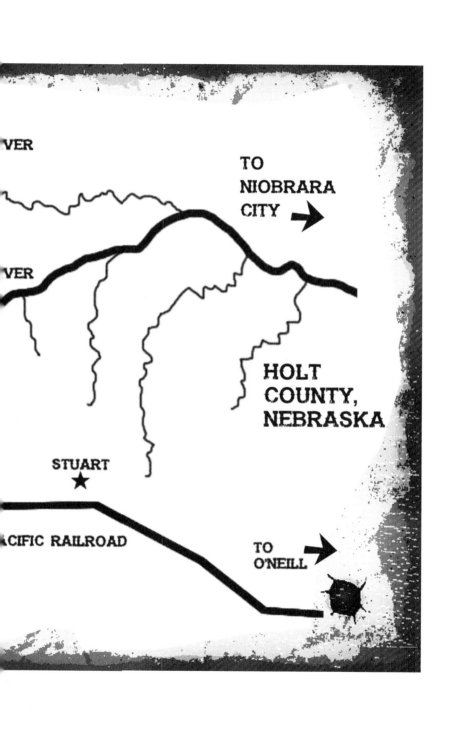

CHAPTER ONE

At the end of October, around the same time winter came back to the north rugged hills of Nebraska, I watched Virgil Manke's spotted paint bangtail outrun Ben Frymire's Kentucky bay mare under a pair of heavy pine trees at Long Pine Creek near Seven Springs. I kept company with Sonny Clausen and Henry Richardson, and the nearby forest made a dark silhouette against a blue curtain of storm clouds.

I wore a suit because I was in Long Pine with Sonny on business, buying canyon timber from Manke. My collar was starched and itchy, and it pestered my neck something fierce. I dug at the stiff attire, fingers brushing against my sandy brown hair curling long over my shoulders. I guess the jacket kept me warm enough.

Manke's track across the grassy meadow was wet from an afternoon shower, and the horses chewed the damp loam to oatmeal. I prayed nobody turned a hoof.

Sonny sipped rum from a ceramic crock and encouraged his jockey toward the finish. "Push her, you sonuvabitch!" Sonny wore what he always wore, wool pants and a long-sleeved cotton shirt over the top of his long underwear. Didn't matter if it was summer or winter, the only two seasons we have up here, Sonny was comfortable.

Neither one of us carried a hat, but I wished I did because Virgil Manke had a dandy bowler and Frymire fancied his Stetson. I liked rubbing elbows with monied equestrians. Bareheaded, I stood a little lower than them.

Manke's Miss Baghdad was wild and quick, and Sonny had ten dollars bet on her.

When she beat Frymire's Shady Jane, he 'bout choked up a lung.

"I had hopes, August John," he told me. "I had hopes, but — oh, my stars — I never believed it. I never believed I would win. Not in a million years of Sundays." He smelled like sweat and rum and piss the way some old men do, but he won close to twenty dollars when that pacer pounded over the line. Financially, he was better off than me.

"You still know your horseflesh, Sonny," I

said, patting his back. "Now, go get your winnings."

It was old Henry Richardson who'd encouraged Sonny to place his bet. "Did I tell you, Clausen? Or did I tell you?"

"You're right about it, Henry." He still couldn't believe it. "You both told me true."

Sonny's expression made me laugh out loud. "Will you just go get your money before they hand it to somebody else?"

Sonny beamed with success. "Boys, I know horses better'n anybody. But, I never believed we'd win today, let alone so much money." He shook his head, honestly surprised at his good fortune. And he really did know horses. He could recognize a horse by her prints in the sod.

"You go collect your winnings," I said again.

"I'm gonna do just that. C'mon, Henry." The two walked off together to join a ring of happy gamblers gathered around Miss Baghdad. Sonny said, "See you later, August John."

I took off my string tie, stuffed it into my pocket, and tugged at the itchy collar again.

I still wished I had a hat.

Sonny's the only one who still calls me August John, a name I buried with my career as a horse thief five years gone and

11

more. Now I was just John Augustus — friends called me Gus — watching the half-mile race with a dozen other folks, jawboning like partygoers do when chance throws them together, on a restful Thursday afternoon. From the looks of things Manke had invited all of Brown County, plus a few easterners from Holt and Knox.

Sonny Clausen was a pal from those bad old days, longer in the tooth than my old man but with the benefit of still drawing breath. Sonny and my pap had served together at Fort Randolph, though I never really knew my dad, and my mom . . . she could go hang.

I looked up to Sonny in ways I never could understand because, Good Lord! — the damned yapping cuss could get under your skin. I still don't understand it.

Sonny was near eighty years old, with rheumy yellow eyes and puffy vein-mapped skin, and he didn't walk straight. Back when Sonny lived in Paddock, and when Pleasant Valley was a store for local homesteaders, he carried in wholesale goods to me and Trudy, my wife. That was in the days before the railroad came to Long Pine and made it a regional hub for dry goods and produce.

Having no kin of his own left, Sonny now stayed with Trudy and me at Pleasant Valley, and I watched out for him — parent to a man three times my age and then some. Not the kind of father I wanted to be, but life doesn't often give you a choice.

In turn, Sonny wrangled deals for me, like the wagonload of cut cedar and pine I'd purchased from Virgil Manke.

I checked my pocket watch and saw the day was near lost. Lightning laced the southern sky, and thunder followed along. A warning.

Across the Niobrara River on one of the tributaries of the Keya Paha, Pleasant Valley was a far piece north from Manke's spread where Sonny and I sat without slickers. And us low on tobaccy.

When a big gust of wind came rolling up from that batch of cauliflower clouds on the horizon, I was in a hurry for Sonny to shake Manke's fat hand so we could leave with our wagonload for home.

I didn't love the idea of freighting all that wood in the rain, nor traversing Long Pine Creek Canyon twenty-plus miles to where it opens to the wide Running Water valley.

Near the horse race finish line, stroking his waxed fat mustache, white-haired Virgil Manke was pampered with attention from a slew of grinning livestock barons. There was Cap Burnham from Carns, and C.C. Dodge

13

stood alongside Henry Richardson's nephew, Ted Roberts. Ted worked for Manke as a hand and lived here on his ranch.

Manke wore a big wool coat and kid gloves and waited for his jockey to swing Miss Baghdad back around. His coat looked awfully expensive. But I guess it cut the wind better than my jacket.

Sonny was right up front, running off at the mouth, "What a show! What a trotter!"

I took a few steps back away from everybody else.

On the far side of the mud, Ben Frymire was being a good loser, leading Shady Jane around toward the bunch with his boy who rode the mare into second place. The old devil was everything Manke wasn't — broomstick thin and leather tough wearing jeans and a light, long-sleeved shirt. Frymire was a bachelor sodbuster whose dad immigrated from Norway to Bassett, a few miles east of Manke's spread. His pa had kicked off early and left a young kid to grow old alone with his ma on Nebraska dirt.

A kraut farmer clapped his shoulder, "Better luck next time, Ben," and wandered off toward Manke's enormous white house.

"Thanks," Frymire said, and while he talked with the boy, his hat wagged back

14

and forth like it might make a jump at any second.

I knew Virgil Manke from the Long Pine auction barn since he ran cows along with horses. Cap Burnham was a local attorney with an interest in livestock. Trudy knew Manke, too — but from longer ago, when she ran guns for Doc Middleton and us Pony Boys and whoever else had folding money or gold.

Manke had his fingers in everything for as long as I could remember.

Sonny clutched his winnings in hand and gushed all over Mr. Manke. "I sure enough thank you for asking us to stay over this afternoon. God knows I've been awful unlucky of late. God knows it. I guess I was owed something."

Manke brushed him off quick, but friendly enough. "Well, Sonny, I was glad to help you boys out with that wood. Call again, soon, won't you?"

"Yes, sir. By God, next time we're here, we'll look you up. We certainly will do that."

Sonny never knew a stranger, and while them clouds boiled up mad, pregnant with a lake of water and ice, I liked to think he'd never get a move on, him showing his wad of bills to each of the other men. Some of them had won money too, of course.

I shoved my hands deep in my hip pockets and played with my folding knife and wondered if — as long as I was hanging around waiting — maybe I oughtn't have a drink. Maybe something to eat before we took to the road.

Manke's wife and daughters had a lunch laid out in front of the house behind us on linen gray tablecloths, mostly deviled eggs and ham sandwiches, but there was a barrel of beer at the far end of the spread. The kraut farmer was there now filling his mug.

With Miss Baghdad beating out Shady Jane, there'd likely be a hell of a good party in the offing, even if the weather forced everybody to move inside. Maybe Sonny and me should stay a while, after all? A beer would taste awfully good.

While I tried to make up my mind, a stick figure with a fancy claw-hammer coat, gray britches, braces, and black hat slipped out from behind one of the cottonwoods. The sneaky fellow was on his way toward Manke's congratulatory crowd, and I guess he wasn't expecting me to be standing there because he flinched when he saw me.

That's just what he did, *flinched,* and his hand worried the big nickel-plated six-shooter drooping off his hip.

And me with nothing but a dime-store

16

knife tucked away in my trousers.

"How do," I said, with a cautious nod.

He lifted his chin. "How do."

The short man's eyes were dry, hard stones, his jaw clenched around a smoking cigarette in a grimace that made me sad.

That first time seeing Albert Wade back from jail, I figured he'd give me a smile. Guess I figured wrong. His eyes were flat, the smile muscles in his face looked to be atrophied from lack of use.

I stood a good many inches taller than him, always had, but right about then he looked like he could lick me and the whole entire world combined. I cleared my throat.

"Good race, eh?"

"Seen better."

"You put any money on them trotters?"

"Who's asking?" He took a last big draw off his smoke and dropped it smoldering to the ground.

"I was just curious." I pointed my chin at Miss Baghdad. "She's a real peach."

With patches of snow-white hair over a field of sandy brown, the mare moved like a silk hanky under the hands of the surrounding men, and her dusty beige tail was a defiant statement, uncombed.

Albert was noncommittal. "She's all right."

Somebody had sliced an apple into quarters, and Manke took great delight at rewarding the horse. Relishing the treat with a toss of her head and a straight line of teeth, Miss Baghdad made everybody laugh, showing off and swishing her tail.

"I think she's a fine horse," I said. "Makes me think of Chief Spotted Tail's remuda. Remember that pinto you roped in Dakota?"

"Spotted Tail's dead, and you got me mixed up with somebody else. My name's *Sam Gordon.*"

Which was stupid because I knew who he was, and he knew who he was, and that was Albert Wade, called "Kid Wade" and "Slippery Jack" and stepson of John Wade, one-time confederate of Doc Middleton and Curley Grimes and the rest of us Pony Boys, and a fellow I used to trust with my life.

But again, just like with Trudy and her guns, that was a long time before now.

"Whatever you say. I guess I'm pleased to know you, Sam Gordon," I said with a laugh. "How long you been back?"

But Albert wasn't having it, and his dead eyes sent a freeze into my guts.

"I don't know what you're talking about, mister."

He said it just like that, like everything we

18

ever lived and shared together wasn't worth the cigarette butt he dropped to the ground and twisted under his boot.

For a while, we stood in silence as we watched Frymire brush down his horse. Shady Jane followed her owner's lead with gentle humility, her coal-black legs strong, long, and whipsaw lean, speckled with debris of sandy loam. Her rust brown coat showing off a smooth polish that rippled with light as she moved.

"Jane's a good-looking horse too," I said. "Wouldn't mind having her for myself. How about you?"

Al curled his lip and, spinning on his heel, dismissed our whole damn conversation with a snooty nod. He started to walk away, but I called after him.

"Albert, wait."

But the ornery cuss kept right on walking, crossing the ground between me and Manke's cronies, passing Sonny Clausen without giving him a look. Sonny was too delirious over his money to notice the infamous personage passing him by.

"Looky, looky, looky," he said, trotting toward me, waving his paper dole in the air. "Heeeee-hee, we got enough here for a dozen new jugs o' hootch."

Over Sonny's shoulder, I saw Albert shake

hands with Manke, and he jerked a thumb toward Miss Baghdad while another gust of wind forced most of the men to turn their back. Manke shook his head, no, but his expression stayed pleasant enough.

Al persisted, now waving his hands around, moving his shoulders and chin.

I'd seen the old play enough times to imagine the words of "Sam Gordon."

"She's a mighty fine, horse, sir. Mighty fine. What'll you take for her?"

"Sorry, son, Miss Baghdad's not for sale."

"Everything's for sale if the money's right. C'mon. I'll give you $100."

"Twice that's an insult." Manke wagged his thick head of hair and grinned like a schoolboy. "How about I show you some of my other stock?"

"I'll go $110."

"I'm sorry, son. Like I say, I've got some other racing stock over in the barn. If you're truly in the market, I'd be happy to show you those."

"Make it $115. My final offer for the mare?"

Manke shook his head, but he put his arm around the jailbird's shoulders. His words were plain as day then, carried on the wind of the storm. "Come see my sorrels, Mr. Gordon. I got six to choose from."

And old "Sam" agreed with a look of fake gratitude — the same one we'd practiced on each other during supper in the Sandhills or when swapping swaybacks for hot blood mares with Germans on the Keya Paha.

Kid Wade said, "Don't mind if I do take a look. Don't mind if I do."

"You see who that was?" I said.

Sonny looked around like waking up from a dream. "Who was who?"

"That banty rooster shuffling away with Manke toward the barn."

"I never seen him before."

"What if I told you that was Albert Wade?"

"I'd say Kid Wade was buried deep in the Iowa Men's Reformatory at Anamosa and good riddance to him."

"I guess somebody turned the key and let him run. He's calling himself Sam Gordon, now."

Sonny shrugged like it didn't matter beans to him, and why should it? He was an old duffer, and the skeletons in his closet had already turned to dust. Too bad that wasn't the case for everyone.

"Let's get us something to eat," he said. Thunder rolled overhead, and the ladies at the serving tables turned their faces up to the uninvited clouds. Like a stern look would chase them away. "I could use a drink," Sonny said.

"You've been drinking all afternoon, you damned spoonbill."

If Sonny felt an ounce of shame, he didn't show it. "Don't tell me a little dose wouldn't taste good before we take to the road back home?"

Even without the rain, it was bound to be a lonely trek in the dark. We wouldn't see Pleasant Valley until well after midnight.

Sonny said, "Cold as it is, them clouds could bring along some snow. We'd do well to fortify ourselves."

"Since you put it that way, lead on."

Sonny took my arm, and we marched toward Manke's three-story frame house, just a few steps ahead of the other guests. Over at the gambrel-roofed barn, Manke loitered with Albert inside one of the double half-doors. The barn was half again as tall as my shed at Pleasant Valley and painted a bright scarlet red trimmed in ivory. At the top, a tin cupola and rooster-topped weather vane finished the homey picture.

I said, "Virgil's Miss Baghdad isn't his only racehorse, is it?"

"No, sir," Sonny said, "He's got at least four others in there, one out of Boss Ryley over at O'Neill." Which was something to say because Boss Ryley was one of General O'Neill's own line of old studs. "Virgil Manke's serious about his racing."

"I heard him say something about some sorrel horses," I said.

"He's only got part of the sorrels, and the other part belongs to Henry Richardson."

"I see."

Henry was one tough bird, and he'd been Doc Middleton's father-in-law up until Doc went to jail. Not long after that, Henry's daughter, Mary, who everybody called Pood, divorced him and went off to marry somebody else.

I'd heard Doc was out of jail now too.

Unlike some folks, I guess he'd learned a lesson, because he hadn't come back around the area.

While Sonny loaded his plate up with eggs and biscuits, I watched Albert follow Manke into the dark of the barn. I couldn't see or hear anything going on inside, but I knew Albert never purchased a horse fair and square in his life, and I didn't figure him to start now.

It twisted up my guts to think of him starting up again with the horse thieving.

So much so that when Sonny shoved a plate of chow under my nose, I passed it up. "Just gimme something wet," I said.

23

And once I got started at the crock, I couldn't stop thinking about Doc and Kid Wade. Couldn't stop remembering my poor old pal Dill Schiller hanging purple and rotten from an old tree branch. Or how Otto Randolph's vigilantes had almost put me in the ground with his other victims.

Then the clouds broke open, and the sky fell down with big flakes of snow and ice, and I didn't stop drinking for a long, long time.

CHAPTER TWO

The morning after Virgil Manke's horse race, me and Sonny Clausen plodded into Pleasant Valley before the dawn — stinking drunk, soaked to the bone, and riding a wagon full of cut, snow-covered timber behind Levi, my old Percheron. Following our bashful trickle of a stream, we came to the long house with its privy, our gable-roofed barn, and the circle corral out front in its perpetual state of decline. Trudy's dog, Moses McGee, came charging through dirty slush to meet us, a rolling ball of hair trailing slobber and frozen slop.

Shivering, Sonny and me dragged the lazy sun into the sky, singing dirty songs, and we drove through our chickens, leaving them flustered and clucking.

"A is for Ass, upon which we sit. B is for Balls, each man has a pair. C is for —"

"Cross."

In the first morning light, Trudy stood in

25

the doorway of our two-room home, hands on her hips and wide awake. God-awful early. Like she'd been up all night.

Dressed for the day in men's corduroy pants and a loose cotton shirt coat.

Dressing us down like kids.

"Where the hell have you two been?"

"Uh-oh," Sonny said with a snicker. "Somebody's in trouble." Then he elbowed me in the ribs.

"You s'pect it's us?"

"I s'pect it might be."

I put my hand over my heart. "I'm sorry we're late, dear."

Trudy was too irritated with me to answer. She hated me being gone from home, and she hated it even more when I was late coming back.

But something else was wrong too. I could tell from the awkward tilt of her hip and the crooked curl of her slender lips.

"D is for Dung, what the farmers call —"

I nudged Sonny to shut it.

"Cross is the mood she's in," I said.

Trudy shot me the skunk eye. "That's a polite way to put it."

As usual, Sonny couldn't put a cork in it. "Or maybe it's Jesus's cross. Maybe she's sayin' we need saliva . . . salivatation?"

"The only *salvation* for you, Sonny

Clausen, is to sweat out your rum under a hot sun."

Trudy was religious about reading her Bible, and my head hurt just thinking about a hot sun.

Sonny grinned. "Lucky for me, we ain't liable to get much more summer for a while."

On a chilly autumn day not so unlike this one, Trudy Haas and I had tied the knot in the tree-lined cut full of gnarled blueberry and elm, south of the Keya Paha, but north of the Running Water, what the Indians called the Niobrara River. Trudy named the scrub-filled acreage with its short forest and little crick Pleasant Valley Station. Sonny, along with a teamster named Timmons, had brought in goods every few days from Paddock and Stuart, and Trudy sold 'em at retail prices to homesteaders.

During the years at Pleasant Valley, I tried to keep up with the split-rail corral and barn. Kept a few heifers pastured nearby.

Life was good enough. But there wasn't a lot of shade in the heat of the day. Trudy wore out a good many sunbonnets.

"I was never one to mind winter," Sonny said. "In fact, I rather enjoy it."

"Ain't you something else?" I said.

"My ma always said so, seein's as I'm half Ponca Indian."

Sonny's lineage changed as need be to the fit the story.

I climbed down from the wagon, careful not to tumble when the world swayed, and I landed on my bootheels, fair and square.

Trudy shoved a list of chores at me. "You might as well get started."

"How about after some breakfast?" My head started to throb. "Too much beer, not enough devil's eggs."

Sonny said, "You mean it the other way around."

Trudy helped him down from the wagon. "I've got a list for you too, old man."

He turned his back on her. "I'm a'goin' to bed."

The barn was little more than a twenty-foot-tall stack of driftwood with mud between the boughs, piled high with a gable tin roof spilling down the west side to add an extra slope over a low-flying lean-to I'd added on for calves. It looked as lopsided as my drunken balance, and I figured the new timber we carried back from Long Pine would go a long way to shore up the frame.

I admired Sonny's fortitude living in there without complaints.

Trudy clucked her tongue and watched him waddle toward the stable space he shared with our milk cow, Betty.

I stretched my spine, then made a fist and dug my knuckles into my aching back, caught a glance of Trudy's sun-brown face, speckled with freckles, framed by shoulder-length dark hair, and it seemed just the cure to my long, miserable ride.

"Give us a smooch," I said. She had strong shoulders and small, firm breasts, and my arms fit snug around her waist.

"You'll get a smooch after you've tended to the list of chores," Trudy said, twisting away from me.

And there it was again — the *something else* she wasn't saying.

She was annoyed by Sonny and me showing up late, but there was more to it than that. I knew from the stiff carriage of her legs, the set of her hip. She wasn't one to get riled up easy.

I combed a strand of her hair back, hooked it behind her ear.

"Awww, heck. I'll do all this stuff tomorrow. Tomorrow's Friday."

"Today's Friday."

I nuzzled her graceful jawline. "Aw, c'mon."

"Gus, you know —"

Before she could finish, Moses McGee leapt to his paws and sounded off the alarm. He wasn't all that brave, but his bark could peel the paint off a whitewashed fence. The mutt whirled around in a circle, a knee-high patchwork of coarse black, white, and brown fur — fifty pounds of confusion. He was Trudy's dog before us, and I never really took to him.

Trudy jumped like a ghost goosed her butt, and I spun around to inspect the road we came in on.

But there was nothing there.

McGee barked three times, then skulked around Trudy's legs, whining.

"What's got him so jumpy?" I asked Trudy. "You too?"

"I'm not jumpy." She lied. "McGee's got a botfly in his haunch."

"If you say so." But he didn't have any botfly, not at this time of year.

"Hey, August Jooohhhn. Heeey!"

Sonny trudged back in our direction from inside the barn, rubbing the back of his head, his voice full of gray confusion. "Betty's gone. What happen' to Betty?"

"I dunno," I said. "Something happen to Betty?"

Sonny said, "She's gone. Your buckskin is there, but Betty's gone. Her pen is open, and she's — poof — vanished, like that." Tongue at his lips, he worked to snap his fingers.

Trudy said, "I was going to tell you later."

"Tell me what?"

Sonny concentrated on making his fingers work, but every time he got them lined up to snap, his thumb slipped away. He whispered under his breath, "Poof."

Trudy said, "I guess you better come inside our house."

Her house. Even when she called it ours, it was hers.

No matter how comfortable I felt in the cedar-beam domicile, twenty feet wide and the length of two wagon-teams, it belonged to her in my mind. She lived there first, she claimed it, and I just happened to move in after making my wedding vows. I called it home, but she and McGee and Betty the cow had deep roots in the hardpan floor. Glass windows were my only contribution during the past couple years.

Folks thought she homesteaded the claim with a drummer from back east, but it was John Wade, her cousin on her mother's side — Kid Wade's stepfather.

Him and Albert, and the Kid's mother, Deborah, used to have a place over by Big Sandy Creek. I didn't know where John and Deborah lived now.

Albert had no use for his step-rooster — that's what he called him, *step-rooster.* And

Trudy hated John Wade for the way he had abused her.

Which is why it knocked me back in my chair when she brought up his name.

"It's about Wade," she said, and I knew who she meant.

Trudy poured steaming coffee with chicory from the tin pot on the stove and put down the ceramic cups in front of Sonny and me. My stomach made a rolling petition for breakfast or the outhouse, I wasn't sure which, and I sipped real careful from the hot lip of my cup.

After trying to talk to Albert in Long Pine, I was all riled up myself.

"John Wade installed that shiny water pump out front," Sonny said.

Trudy confirmed it. "Yes, and on the day he left me for good, he dropped a heifer calf on my doorstep. That calf grew up to be Betty," she said. "Our milk cow."

"Sounds like the old boy had a guilty conscience," Sonny said.

Trudy said, "We got three calves out of Betty. We'll get more after we breed her to Frymire's Angus bull."

I was tired of her knocking around the main question. "What happened to Betty? Where is she? And what's it got to do with John Wade?"

"John took Betty away. He came last night and took her back."

"Took her? Hold on here." I pushed myself up, away from the round oak dining table we sat around. "Are you saying Wade was *here*? Albert's dad was here at Pleasant Valley?"

"Stepdad."

I ignored the correction and kept on. "What made that bastard come sniffing around here?" My temper burned off all the leftover rum in my blood. I never felt more sober in my life. "You didn't send word for him or some fool such thing?"

Trudy's reaction was instant, like I'd slapped her in the face. "Gracious, no."

"Then what did he want?"

"I don't know what he wanted. I don't think he knew either."

"He didn't say?"

"He said a lot of things, but none of it made sense. It's not like he wanted anything at first. It was more like he was just making sure."

"Making sure of what? That he wasn't welcome here? That you still curse his name?"

"I think he was making sure about you."

"And he settled for stealing Betty," I said.

"Maybe he was looking for horses. Like

33

the Kid, down at Manke's place," Sonny said.

"Kid Wade?" Trudy said, half rising from her chair. "Albert was in Long Pine?"

I waved her back into her chair.

"He showed up at Virgil Manke's horse race," I said. "Totin' a big six-shooter, nosing around the barnyard."

Sonny said, "I'll bet there's something going on between them. Why else would these two buzzards all of a sudden show up at the same time."

The muscles around the base of my skull bunched up tight like a vice, and my shoulders were tight. I glared at Trudy. Even though I knew it wasn't her fault, I started sweating her. "You tell me everything you can remember about Wade's visit. Tell me everything he said."

The thought of John Wade being alone with her . . .

For the first time, I noticed the iron-colored bruises on her forearm. Small, indistinct, but close together. Like she'd been grabbed, caught up in a man's grip.

I noticed the rip in the shoulder seam of her sweater.

"Tell me what he said."

Trudy said, "Is it so important —"

And I bit off her words like a trapped

34

coon, snapping at her fingers. "Yes, god-dammit! Yes, it is important." A coon sick with the hydrophobia. *"You tell me right now what happened."*

Sonny said, "If you two need me to leave —"

"You stay right where you are, old man."

Trudy lifted her chin, let her eyes slide over Sonny and me, back and forth. Finally, she said, "Gus is right, Sonny. You should stay. You should hear this too."

"I'm waiting," I said.

Truth was, it felt good to release the anger, and if it was hurtful, I didn't care, because somehow, somewhere deep inside, I blamed her.

Trudy was older than me, past thirty. She'd been with John Wade — in a Biblical way — before she was with me.

Hell if I wasn't still jealous about that.

But that ain't all of it, either.

I was scared.

Trudy said, "He showed up alone just as the sun went down. Loped around the front of the house for a while before knocking on the door."

"You saw him ride in? What kind of horse?"

"A pitiful broke-down nag. I swear, you could see her ribs. Truth to tell, he wasn't looking much better than the horse."

"You let him in the house?"

Here, Trudy got the tough, defiant expression I knew so well. "I did not let him in the house. I walked outside with the scattergun and asked what he wanted."

"Bet he didn't like that," Sonny said. "You pullin' iron on him."

"No, he didn't like it one darned bit. That's when he reached out to snatch my arm. Got a good bite too, but I shoved the gun in his face." Her eyes gleamed with the memory. "He backed off real quick."

I said, "How long did you talk to him?"

"Long enough to tell him to git."

"And then you went back inside the house, and he took the cow?"

She spread both of her hands out flat on the table. "That's all there was to it."

I shook my head. "There's something else. Something you ain't saying."

Lower eyelids brimming with tears, Trudy held her front teeth together, hissing, "Just let it go, okay?"

Whatever it was had to come out.

Again, she said, "Just let it go."

Hunched down over the table like that, she strained to keep it inside, worked her jaw back and forth so she wouldn't explode. I loved her then more than ever before, because I knew — I mean, I really realized, she was keeping quiet for me.

She was trying to protect me.

"Tell me what he said."

"All right." She came out of her seat at me, spring-loaded. "You want to know what John Wade was doing here? I said before, he was making sure about you."

"Making sure we were still together?"

"Making sure you didn't want to join him. He wants you back in the horse-stealing life. He wants you to ride with him."

Sonny whistled with glee. "Glory, hallelujah."

Trudy said, "Could you just put a cob in it for once, Sonny?"

He scoffed, "Like hell."

I said, "Wade must be crazy to come here and ask you that."

"He says if you aren't with him, you're against him."

"He's got that right."

"He said . . ."

Two tears lined her cheek. There was no way to blink 'em off or hold them back.

Watching her wavering between rage and fear stuck like a bug floundering in the mud; my mad was lost, spent, drained away.

I could only eke out a few words, "What? What else did he say?"

"He said if you don't ride with him, he'll shoot you like a pig and trail your guts from here to Niobrara City."

Sonny clapped his hands. "Whoo-wee! Let him try, I say. Let the sumbuck give it a go."

I walked around the table and put my arms around Trudy's shoulders while she buried her face in my shirt.

Eventually, Sonny spoke up, "We won't let him get away with it. We'll show him, won't we, Gus?"

Trudy pushed herself back into her chair, and I let loose of all the air I'd been holding in, and said, "I guess I don't have much of a choice."

"No," Trudy said, "We don't have a choice at all."

After lunch, I went to the corral and cinched a saddle tight around my buckskin gelding, a two-year-old I called Ed. Then I walked back into the barn for my blanket roll and coffeepot. I didn't know how long I'd be on the trail after John Wade, but I figured I might have to make a campfire or three.

I checked the leather rifle boot affixed to Ed's saddle, made sure the carbine there was seated snug, then stepped up and swung myself into the saddle.

Ed felt strong under me. Ready to go.

"Make sure the Percheron gets plenty of water today. I don't want him getting run-down after pulling that wood home yesterday."

Trudy said, "When will you be back?"

More than anything, I wanted to answer her.

I wanted to jump off the horse and take her up in my arms and tell her I wasn't leaving. I wanted to tell her how much I'd missed her when I was away in Long Pine, and how much I cherished every second of our life in the valley.

I wanted to tell her how much I loved her.

And too, I wanted to tell her I'd be back when John Wade was dead.

Or I wouldn't be back at all.

But having so much to say, I said nothing at all and nudged Ed forward, toward our empty, weed-filled corral and then the road beyond.

CHAPTER THREE

Things had changed in the Niobrara River valley since Doc Middleton's day.

By the autumn of 1883, the wild country west of Holt County was getting organized. Brown County was carved out of Holt and Long Pine precinct, early in the year, and though we still didn't have any officials in place, the plan was set, the boundaries drawn. The railroad reached Stuart and Bassett and then on to Valentine. Every other hill had a new immigrant family cutting into the sod, and fresh produce, dry goods, and everyday tools were common and easy to procure from Long Pine on the rail line.

Some folks thought the Sioux would rise up when Crow Dog killed Spotted Tail in '81, and that was a terrible rough winter with cold and snow. But two years later, from Pleasant Valley east to where the Keya Paha mates with the Niobrara in vast,

40

sprawling congress, life was flourishing.

Telegraph lines ran between the cities, and newspapers — Lord, the newspapers! — were everywhere with their blaring headlines.

Progress, every place you looked.

But sometimes, especially when I was alone and trotting over an open range, when the bluestem grass was dry and gone to seed and rippled like long, slow ocean waves in the afternoon wind, I'd catch myself reliving the days when nothing could touch me.

Not friends. Not women. Not love.

Least of all, the law.

What law? In the unorganized territories on the Niobrara tributaries, we did as we pleased.

With friends now gone — some to green fields and some to heaven — Albert Wade and me and Dill Schiller borrowed ponies from the Sioux and the old Ponca agency, flipped 'em to farmers and stockmen, turned around, and did it again and again.

Storybook kings, we imagined ourselves above the peasants who lived along the Running Water. Devils without worry, we didn't care who got hurt.

We had a hell of a lot of fun. But it wasn't a healthy way to live.

Sometime along the way, I turned around

and pledged myself to Trudy — and hadn't we made good on our life since those sordid times? We had the house and the barn, the horses and cows. We had each other. Maybe more in the future.

What else was there but the promise of good times ahead? What else could we possibly need?

Improvements to the house and barn.

A passel of kids.

Wasn't it good to keep my nose polished clean?

And now this filthy sonuvabitch John Wade wanted to trespass in my paradise. Wanted to bring his scruffy behind into my home and pull me over backwards.

No.

Some men couldn't take a piss without their past coming back to sock 'em a good one. That wasn't me. Not after I'd worked so hard to make a different life for myself.

I followed the familiar snaky trail down the creek canyon to Long Pine, same as the day before.

Alone in the saddle, I made good time as the snow melted to mud along the road.

Carns wasn't more than a wide spot in the road with Tarbell's shop, some hasty shanties, a few cottonwood trees, and the trail to Morris's Bridge over the river. I stopped to ask about John Wade. The only man around was Jim McFarlin behind his post office station. "Ain't seen nobody," he said, maybe a little too fast.

I never liked Jim, and the way he answered made the hairs on my arms stand up straight.

"Cap Burnham around?" I said. "I know his place is nearby, and he stops in to the store now and again." My thinking was if I could talk to a big man like Cap about what happened, he'd be sympathetic and share news a regular fella like me wasn't overly privy to. Sometimes men like him kept track of men like Wade. For the well-being of all.

McFarlin surely had nothing good to say. "You think I'm Burnham's wet nurse?"

I couldn't believe he'd talk that way — wet nurse! — so I left the store.

You couldn't even be nice to the sorry bastard. I mean, who talks such a way?

I punched around a fair bit, looked into a couple shacks along the road, hoping somebody might come along to talk to.

At one of the shacks, I leaned on the doorjamb a while and tossed rocks into a tin can, wondering where to go next. I counted three wasp nests under the eave and squeezed one between my thumb and forefinger when the first one brushed against my head. The remnants of summer.

It was mighty lonesome country.

After a while, I got tired of waiting to see if anybody would show, so I crossed Morris's timber bridge — it made a clip-clopping echo against the water — and followed the mushy trail south toward Manke's place where I'd seen Albert calling himself Sam Gordon. The bridge wasn't too old, only a few years, but a bigger mess of bent square nails and shivering support trusses I'd never seen. Still and all, it held together thirty more years until the ice jams finally took it out.

That day in October I planned on keeping a steady pace, not push Ed too hard, but not let him loaf, either. Sonny knew horses, and so did I. I lived long enough with both of 'em. First horse I took a real liking to was called Prince — as in "unprincipled." A gorgeous chestnut, he was sneaky in a lot of ways. Any chance he got, he would laze around like a schoolkid in May.

So far, Ed wasn't like that.

The next people I met on my route were a pair of Ponca Indians hiking through Long Pine Creek Canyon on their way to Atkinson. A man and his daughter. *"Aho,"* I said, which is saying hello in Indian, but I don't know if I pronounced it right. These two dressed like white pioneers out of a history book with suspenders and straw hats probably 100 years old.

They hadn't seen John Wade, but the daughter said she knew who he was. I don't think she told the truth, but we made a trade of my coffee for some smoked meat. I enjoyed talking to them, since I hadn't seen anyone other than McFarlin all day. I especially like the Ponca language and was happy to practice with them a little before they wanted to move on. I could tell they were getting bored with me.

The dad said, "So long, *ikʰáge*." We parted as friends.

I made camp overnight in a clearing next to a tall scrub-covered butte and had the Indian meat for supper. It was a good trade, and I still had enough coffee to float my back molars. Plus, my camp coffee wasn't nearly as good as what Trudy made for us at night.

Sergeant O'Leary's red-cedar cabin was supposed to be around the canyon someplace, and Sonny had said we ought to get some construction tips from him before putting the fresh lumber to work back home. I couldn't see going to all the trouble of chasing after a man for advice on how to pound a nail.

Saturday I climbed out of the creek cut to mosey into town. The storm had blown through the day before with the inevitable frigid cold behind it, but overnight the temperature warmed up some. The next day I was able to ride in my shirtsleeves with my red underwear underneath, my big coat coaxing a sweat.

My first stop was the hotel, to see what was what.

The folks there pretended not to know who John Wade was, and before you knew it, I was back out on the street.

Laid out like a tic-tac-toe grid and rowdy since the train came to town, Long Pine was less than ten years old. Parallel east-west streets numbered one through eight, and the perpendicular ones were named for trees. I had the place mapped out in memory — Tom Moore's feed and flour store, the auction barn, the shoe shop, and the road that led out of town to Manke's place near Seven Springs. It was pretty hard to get lost.

But there was nothing doing there either.

Eventually, I moseyed on east to Bassett, riding up to Martin's Hotel at lunchtime.

I admired the horizontal stained-glass window over the threshold, then walked casually through the doors hoping for something to wet my whistle. First thing, I'm thinking this place needs a good airing out, because it stinks like burned pinfeathers, and then I realize it's on account there's a passel of women crowding the cookstove on the far end doing just that. Singeing pinfeathers. The stained glass made the floor around the entrance bloody red.

"Chicken day, is it?" I said, to nobody and everybody, and who rolls in from a back door but this bum Ted Roberts, nephew to Henry Richardson. Ted's a bit younger than me, but he had grown up well enough. He wasn't so much a bum, but I always called him that. It seemed like he always needed a shave, and I wished I could scrub the eternal mad-red splotch of pimples off his cheek.

Foggy fat spectacles hung from his ears, and a collapsible top hat capped the thick raven hair on his head. "How do, Gus."

"How's Ted, today?" I said.

"I saw you at Manke's race on Thursday. Guess you won a nice pile off Miss Baghdad."

"Sonny did. I don't gamble much."

"That's your loss. You ought to give it a try. I landed quite a reward." Damned if Ted wasn't always trying to get his paw on my butt. He ran a crooked finger along the brim of his hat. "Pure beaver skin," he said.

"You weren't the only one to win," I said.

"I was the only one who laid down a hundred dollars."

"It's nice if you have it to spend."

"You here to buy a bird?" He hopped up on a stool behind the tall walnut counter like he owned Martin's Hotel, but of course he didn't, and I recognized Sara Martin over with the hens. I decided to needle him a little. "You in charge of the place today?"

"Sure, Gus. Can I get you a drink?"

"I'd take a coffee."

"I can pour you something stronger."

"Coffee's fine."

"Suit yourself."

Elias Martin's wife, Sara, had carrot-orange hair and was elbow-deep in chicken guts over beside Ted's aunt.

I guess Sara saw me watching her, so she hollered, "What'cha know, Gus?"

Ted carried over a tin cup, and I thought, what the hell, I'll see what they can tell me.

So I took a big slurp of hot courage and walked toward the ladies. "I know John Wade's on the prod, Sara. The bastard came knocking on Trudy's door Thursday night. Any of you seen him?"

Well, that entire back part of the open, inviting room was reserved for waltzes and

48

parties, and I even saw a wedding there once, with lots of laughing and crying and such. Long talk and gossip and carving up meat fit the space, but there's never been such a quiet as the one that fell after my question boxed their ears. It beat the silence of the grave.

I gave them a little encouragement. "Wade threatened my home. Threatened me. I need to make sure he understands that won't be happening again."

Six old ladies, fingertips to armpits smeared with fat and gristle and blood standing over four gut buckets and a big round table covered in wet newspapers and more than a dozen dead birds — and not one of them had a durn thing to say.

A slippery hunk of gizzard slid down Sara's left hand and plopped to the floor. She cleared her throat, but it was Ted who piped up first. "You want a hunk of sugar for that coffee, Gus?"

I clomped back across the sand-dusted hardwood floor back to him. "I want to know if anybody's heard from old man Wade."

"Maybe we ought to visit alone, just you and me." Ted sniffed and pushed up the nosepiece on his specs. "Let's us go outside."

I said I'd take the sugar, and he poured a big measure into my cup from a little dish. Too much.

I stirred it with my finger, then followed him around the bar and through the back door to the poultry killing ground.

Ted said, "Pull up a seat," but the only place I saw to rest my butt was a blood-soaked maple stump with a dirty hatchet half-buried in the top. The earth around us was littered with feathers and lonesome chicken heads, the beaks caught open in mid-squawk, eyes already fogged over from lying in the sun. I sipped my coffee and watched a black cat pick at one of the heads before carting it off around the corner of the long ranch-style building.

"Looks like everybody in town's eating good tonight," I said.

"Methodist church social tomorrow since the circuit preacher's coming to town," Ted said. "Fried chicken and vinegar cabbage slaw. You'll want to stay over and take it in. Sara's got a sour cream pie tastes like what you know they eat in heaven."

I took a few steps onto the prairie and kicked at a dead Russian bull thistle. It was crooked and dried up and the purple flowers had gone to seed. I never would've bothered it in the summer when a honeybee

50

might've launched up off the blossom and drilled me. But so late in the season, and after a first snow, I felt safe.

"You say you ain't seen John Wade?"

"I didn't say nothing," Ted said. He pulled a sack of flake tobacco from his shirt pocket along with a few rolling papers. "I'd offer you a smoke, but I'm down to three papers."

"I don't mind," I said. "I'm still drinking my coffee."

Ted sprinkled a few flakes on the paper like an old hand, and I marveled at how much the kid had grown up since he ran with Albert and me back around the time Doc Middleton got married. Back then he couldn't keep a thimbleful of whiskey from crawling back up his gullet, and here he was serving hooch at the bar and smoking like a teamster. Now if only he'd take some lye to those nasty damn carbuncles on his face.

Once Ted was lit and puffing, I got real serious.

I figured maybe we'd danced enough and the soft shoe was over. Time for a boot on the butt.

"Listen, Ted, we go back a long time. But nobody threatens me on my own property. Nobody lays a hand on my wife. Any man does that has to answer for it. Same way for any man who protects such a rascal."

I let that last comment sink in, and I could tell Ted was chewing it all over because the ash on his curly grew long like a worm before he thought to knock it off.

"Thursday night, you say?"

"Thursday night."

Ted shook his head. "Thursday night ain't a good thing to talk about around Long Pine. You saw how them gals in there reacted when you mentioned it."

"When I mentioned John Wade."

He brushed my words aside like they didn't have a lot of meaning. "Naw, Wade don't mean so much by himself. It's because you said Thursday night along with saying his name."

"What happened Thursday night?"

"Six horses from over at Virgil Manke's place went missing."

I have to admit, the news hit me square between the eyes. I'd seen Albert with my own eyes. Talked to him, suspected he was up to no good. But I didn't expect him to work so fast.

"Does Manke have any idea who did it?"

"Six thoroughbred sorrels gone like they never were there. Saddles and bridles too."

I imagined Sonny snapping his fingers and whispering. "Poof."

"What about Miss Baghdad?"

"Miss Baghdad is safe and sound. They left her alone."

I said, "I'll bet Manke is fit to be tied."

"He's heartbroke is what he is, Gus. Them sorrels are more than business to him. My uncle Henry Richardson owns part of them. It's about their friendship. Got him sick to the belly and pining."

"I'm awful sorry to hear it."

"The hell of it is," Ted said, "Uncle Henry's got a bug on like you never seen." Then Ted's voice dropped like a lead sinker, and when he spoke, I couldn't quite make out his words.

I had to ask him to repeat what he said. I walked up close so I'd hear him.

Ted flipped his cigarette away, a pinwheeling spiral of sparks. "I said, there's talk of what's to be done."

"What's to be done?" I said.

"Cap Barnham and Manke want to get organized."

"Organized?" For a second, I wasn't sure what he meant. Things were happening faster than I had gotten used to during the slow days I shared with Trudy at Pleasant Valley.

I was out of practice for dark nonsense and furious shenanigans.

Ted said, "An organized group of men."

"You mean a vigilance group?" I said.

"Brown County's dragging ass on getting law officers appointed. It's the same old political bullshit talk, but there ain't no law yet. Not any law anybody can count on."

"I saw Kid Wade at the race. He called himself Sam Gordon, but it was Albert."

"Yeah, I saw him. I saw Tony Pike there, too. Manke says he heard Albert was running with Tony and Willy Ransom. Eph Weatherwax, too. And Culbertson."

I gripped the handle of the hatchet, yanked it free of the maple, and let it drop to the ground.

I needed to sit down.

"Pike and Ransom are no good."

"And Eph Weatherwax, you remember we called him White Stockings."

I remembered all too well.

Ted squatted down on his haunches beside the stump while I rested my bones there.

"It's what Manke heard tell is all."

"Manke's pretty sure Albert took the sorrels?"

Ted shrugged and started building another smoke. "Tony Pike approached a settler last week about a mousy dun. He used the name Sam Gordon then, too."

"Dammit," I said. "It's what I was afraid of. There's a whole ring of them working together."

"Something's got to be done, Gus. It ain't like the old days."

I felt like he stepped on my dick there, and said so. "Don't get so cute, pus-face."

Ted couldn't care less if I was mad. He just grinned.

There was a time a little menace in my voice would go a long way to shaking up young Ted, but today he licked his cigarette paper cool as Mother Mary. He was all grown up now.

"You want to get tough, save it for the horse thieves. If Cap Burnham pulls together a crew, you'd be a good man to ride with us."

I said, "That's my second invitation in as many days."

"Somebody else is pulling together a bunch of regulators?"

"Not exactly," I said. Then I told him John Wade wanted me to ride with him too.

"What'd you tell him?"

"What do you think I told him?"

Ted said, "We're meeting at Virgil Manke's house next Saturday. You be there."

After a few minutes more the sun climbed over the top of the building and I started to smell those chicken heads. Ted wasn't saying much more, so I stood up and shook his hand. "I thank you for the coffee."

"You want me to tell Burnham and Manke you'll go along with us?"

"I want somebody to tell me where John Wade is."

"You come to Long Pine next week, we'll get John, the Kid, Pike, and Ransom — the whole scurvy gang. We'll cast a wide loop, Gus, and bring all them bastards to ground. You'll see."

You could tell Ted was happy about it all. Tom-turkey proud to tell me about it all and ask me in with the vigs, like it was me the younger one just now out of short pants.

I looked him in the eye and turned my back without a word.

I'd had enough such foolishness to last a lifetime.

I had one job to do: warn off John Wade.

After that, all I wanted was to be left alone.

CHAPTER FOUR

First thing after I talked to Ted Roberts, I went next door to find Elias Martin.

He was a good man who I'd known half my life. He knew me before I met Albert, and I remembered him as the man who always had a free piece of hard candy for a kid or a cool dipper of water.

A sign on the hotel door said "Gone Fishing," and I guess he was since it was Saturday. Who could blame him. I guess I was fishing too, wasn't I?

I crossed Bassett's shiny, new railroad tracks and stopped at the hastily built station shack. A sign the size of Texas overshadowed everything, listing the arrival and departure times for the train, the price of tickets, and a stern warning to stand clear when the steamer blew into town. The next freighter would come on Wednesday night, so I guess nobody had reason to be milling around.

With Ted's voice buzzing around inside my head, I started to imagine things, like maybe the rest of the rough country was smarter than me, knowing when to lay low with a gang of cutthroat ruffians out on the loose.

Maybe I was asking for trouble?

Manke says he heard Albert Wade's running with Tony Pike and Willy Ransom.

If what Ted said was true, it didn't bode well for any of us. Pike and Ransom were the meanest dudes I'd ever heard tell of. A pile of bodies owed their demise to the pair, and I had always made sure to steer clear of them.

Albert had been sent to the Iowa Men's Reformatory in Anamosa years before, and I wondered if he hooked up with his new friends in jail. Some of his pals I had never heard of before.

The last time I saw the Kid, before the law caught up with him, he looked me in the eye and said we were quits.

He never could tell the truth, not even to save his rotten soul.

I rode around past the meetinghouse where the church social would be and saw they had tables and folding chairs set up on the grass for the Sunday feed. The little white building was set off real pretty with the grass circling it on three sides, and there were flowers planted on either side of the door. One lone woman worked to unfold chairs and arrange them around each table in turn.

Another week or two it'd be too cold for outdoor visiting. Less than two months until Christmas.

I felt sorry for the lady. How did she end up all by herself moving chairs on a Saturday morning?

I'd never been too much for Sunday school, but Trudy studied her Bible every night before dousing the lantern wick. Sometimes she would read to me from Proverbs, which was my favorite because they're lessons from real life, and I guess King David wrote them down in between wars, and you can see he got the message the Good Lord gave him, probably through a lot of lumps and bruises.

What I didn't like was Revelation. I had more than my share of bad visions, and some of them were dead friends twisting on a rope. Any time I saw four men on horseback riding together, I started to get a nervous feeling.

Trudy figured we could start going to Sunday meetings whenever we had a kid to christen into the church, but so far no little ones had come around.

It wasn't for lack of trying.

Trudy was of an age we needed to shake a leg if anything was ever gonna happen. We were pretty regular at keeping at it, bedding down most nights before it was full dark.

I figured with cold weather on the way, we'd have even more reason to snuggle up and stay warm.

I always wanted to have a little Gus or teeny Trudy, somebody to show the world. I wasn't content to let the care and feeding of Sonny Clausen be my only epithet.

"Pity for geezers" ain't a lot to boast about.

The sun was directly overhead, and I had some of the Ponca meat left in my sack, along with a few biscuits and a jar of sorghum. I could fill my canteen from the creek outside of town. My idea was to find a place for lunch near the camp I had used the night before. Once there, I could study on my options, maybe cipher out what to do and where to go next.

John Wade's trail was as stone-cold dead as a bag of rocks, but I wasn't about to give up.

On the way north, I crossed an open spot in a meadow of green grass and dry cow pies. Good enough. I put my blanket roll, still tied in a bundle, under a couple elm trees, close to where a big cottonwood soaked her feet in a nearby mossy cow pond.

The ground was less damp than the night before, and all the snow had melted off.

Saw a couple Herefords grazing off to the west, but figured if I didn't bother them, they wouldn't bother me. I didn't worry when I found them bunched up in the pond.

One of the bovines bellered loud enough to shake my eardrum, so I hollered in reply, and we played that game for a while, back and forth.

I figured my best bet was to hoof it on north to Ash Creek where C.C. Dodge had a house. If I didn't find Wade, I could maybe buy a milk cow from Dodge and cross the big river there.

If I got going within the hour, I'd be sure to be at Dodge's place before suppertime.

Maybe I should've talked Ted Roberts out of one of them chickens to barter for a calf.

I decided to let Ed rest and munch some grass awhile, figuring I'd stretch out and study on the rest of my plan.

I tipped my hat down to cover my eyes from the sun.

Next thing I know, my ribs are caved in, cracking, and I'm hollering out loud in agony, rolling sideways, skittering away across the loam, a twisting, writhing snake, ducking the moving shadows coming my way. The biggest shade blotted out the sun.

"What's a matter, little runt? You been lookin' for John Wade. Ain't you happy you found him?"

The voice came at me from all sides — deep and guttural like a retching, gagging cough wrapping itself around words half-slurred.

More than the impact, I felt myself moved again, and then a blinding white-hot pain raced up my side to bounce around my lungs and slice into my heart. Flipping over to my butt, I crabbed backwards to the edge of the cow pond trying to keep my balance while raising one hand to shield my eyes from the sun.

If only I could see.

A shadow hovered over me, swaying back and forth, lanky and with a stink of camphor and pig shit and pure grain alcohol.

"W-wade?"

"No happy howdy-do, Gus? No welcome back home?"

John Wade shambled to my left and made a mocking, fake lunge, enough to send me kicking into reverse. When I nearly toppled off the bank into the water, Wade clutched a fistful of my shirt and hauled me back to dry ground, dropping me onto my knees like a sack of oats.

I clutched my side, nursing the ribs he'd kicked with his heavy, pointed boot, not sure if something wasn't broken. Deciding it didn't matter.

This is what I wanted, wasn't it? I brought it on myself, and now I had to fight or die.

Grimacing and doing my best to ignore the fuzzy black patches in my vision that threatened to swallow me up, I climbed to my feet.

Wade stood a ways in front of me, half-drunk, but determined. His eyes were like rolling nuggets of smoldering coal in a skull plastered with flour paste and topped with straw.

"Y . . . you ain't gettin' any better looking with age," I said.

"You got spunk, Gus. I gotta give it to you. But spunk won't save you from me."

I outweighed him by ten pounds, but he had several inches on me. At fifty-plus years he'd seen more of everything than me, including bare-knuckle scraps. His cheeks and neck were fat with scars, and his ears looked mangled and chewed. I glanced at Ed, still content to chew grass with the rifle boot tight to his saddle, the carbine still seated inside.

If I could get that Winchester . . .

My eyes darted back to the fight in time to see Wade whirling toward me, a windmill of arms and outstretched hands. He slapped me across the head, staggered me with the loud crackling thud of the blow. But I stayed upright in my boots, following his attack with a hog-wild pitch back that raked his chin — more luck than any skill at fisticuffs — and surprised him.

Wade rubbed his jaw between finger and thumb. I was stupid enough to think maybe the worst of it was over.

"I came callin' on you the other night, Gus. Thought maybe we could get to know each other better. I guess our Trudy relayed the message."

The inside of my chest felt like it was folding in on itself. I never had anything hurt like that. Struggling with my breath, I said, "She isn't *our* Trudy."

"Oh, sure she is, boy. Us two, we both been with her. Far as I know, you and me are the only ones know the smell of her hair in the rain, the crack in her voice when she's scared. All her little birthmarks, all the ways she can please a —"

Naturally, it was my anger that beat me.

I couldn't stand there and let anybody talk about my wife in such an intimate, ugly way.

No real man could listen to such garbage without protest. And brother, did I protest. My rage scraped the back of my throat raw.

Putting my head down, I drove into Wade's guts, surprising him, pushing him over, toppling him like a moldy oak. I got him straddled like he was a screaming bucking bronco and managed to land a hammer fist right on the bridge of his nose.

I should've been covering my injured ribs.

For Wade to swing his own fist around in a wide arc and crash it into my side was the easiest thing in the world. I almost imagined he whistled while he took his time, leisurely slamming my hot spot over and over, bringing me down to the point of whimpering exhaustion.

I fell sideways off him, and he mounted up on his boots to stand towering above me.

I heard him spit, felt the gob of slimy wet on my cheek.

"You never had a chance, Gus. Like I said, I would've enjoyed getting to know you better. You and Albert being such good pals all them years ago."

I managed a defiant reply. "Albert . . . hates . . . your guts."

"Yeah, yeah. I know it. But the way I hear things, he ain't so fond of you anymore either. I figured if you quit him, maybe you'd rather sign on with the big dogs."

"Big . . . dogs?"

"Too late now. It's all over town what you've been saying. How you're going to make sure I don't come back. How you're gonna teach me a lesson. Keep me from ever seeing my Trudy."

"That's . . . not exactly . . ."

"Not exactly what you said? You sure about that? Because I could've sworn that's the way I heard it."

"From who? Who did you hear it from?"

Wade laughed loud and long. "These folks around here are my friends. My kin. We bartered back and forth for goods and gossip before you were ever born. How about we say a little Bird Lady told me what I wanted to know in exchange for all the white meat I can eat at the church social tomorrow."

Wade scooped up my arm in a grip of iron and dragged me across the field — halfway to Virginia — and I wanted to be sick thinking of him grabbing Trudy, leaving those bruises and hoping that was all that happened.

Then, all I could think of was each blade of grass cut my face like a sharpened steel knife, each thumping gopher mound took my breath away. Before I could get my pins

66

back under me, we were at the edge of the pond, and he slammed me down flat on the bank, facedown in a fetid mossy, mud pile. The cows backed away with slogging indifference. No help at all.

"Thirsty, Gus? Nothing makes you thirsty like a little tussle. Well, ain't you lucky we got a big store of water, right here."

The first time he pushed my head under the surface of the cow pond, I managed to hold my breath. The second time, I swallowed half the pond. The third time I choked and realized I couldn't breathe.

Wade went wild then, laughing and soaking my head in the pond, again and again, for longer spates each time, yammering on about Trudy and his wife, Deborah, and how the only ones who really understood him were the horses.

A forlorn thought — if only I could have reached the Winchester.

If only I hadn't tried to take Wade alone.

In the murky depth of the pond, I saw Ted Roberts's face float up to me, and he kept mouthing the same thing over and over.

If Cap Burnham pulls together a crew, you'd be a good man to ride with.

If only I had a crew.

You come along with us, we'll get John, the Kid, Pike, and Ransom — all of 'em. We'll cast a wide loop, Gus, and bring all them bastards to ground.

I knew I sure couldn't do it by myself.

CHAPTER FIVE

Sick and broken, I laid spread-eagle on the edge of the pond.

When the Herefords bellered, I didn't beller back. It confused them, and they hung around, keeping their distance but no doubt curious to see how and when I would expire.

Those damn cows were probably taking bets on how long I'd last.

I felt myself shuddering, a busted-up pile of bones clattering against the hardpan. But I took comfort in the close proximity of winter. The buzzards had mostly flown the coop south — at least I'd have a nice-looking corpse. Nobody wants their remains torn to shreds.

I shivered through the cold, damp tomb of night, suffered the brightness of the rising sun come morning.

Ed floated around for a while in a dream, nosing me, scrunching his lips on my outstretched arm — the unprincipled louse, begging an apple or lump of sugar. He didn't care beans about me.

That's how I was thinking, if you could call it thought — random weird feelings floating through a dull fog of pain. Nobody cared about me.

By now it was Sunday. Trudy wouldn't care. Did she even miss me?

My guts churned around, and I had to roll to my side to ease the nausea.

But thinking about Trudy is what saved my life.

Imagining John Wade out there, wandering around somewhere, maybe pestering Trudy, and me loafing around like a layabout coon dog. I couldn't smother the croak of his guttural voice inside my head.

Far as I know, you and me are the only ones know the smell of her hair in the rain, the crack in her voice when she's scared.

Fear's the thing what got me moving.

I was more than a little scared of what I'd find when I got home. And I promised myself not to look in a mirror for three weeks.

I didn't so much walk to my horse as pitched myself forward every few feet. A blind tick looking to land on happy horseflesh, tripping over weed traps in the grass

70

and falling all over myself. Once I got ahold of Ed, I couldn't let go, but it took three tries to hoist myself to the saddle, dizzy and gagging, raw from the whipping I took.

My poor head was full of cotton moths, and my lips thick with blisters the size of dung beetles. Riding past Martin's Hotel, I threw up all over my shirt vest.

I felt ashamed of my past. How could I ever have gotten involved with the Wades to begin with? I talked to myself all the way home, and the conversation echoed in the empty cavern of my skull.

Go find the bastard. Shoot him down.
This time you caught a break, Gus.
Tell it to my aching ribs.
Find the bastard.

Having had my lucky ass returned to me from the grim reaper, I didn't know how to be grateful. I wasn't sure that I was.

First, I was afraid that I was going to die. As all the aches and pains took hold, I was afraid I wouldn't die.

The only reason I was alive was John Wade was too lazy to bend down and make sure I was dead.

And now I wanted him to pay for it.

Killing me would've been a mercy.

Trudy's always telling me, "Vengeance is mine, sayeth the Lord," and my answer is that's easy for Him to say.

I forgot about visiting Dodge and followed the rails to Long Pine, then took the well-worn trail back north through Long Pine Creek Canyon, the way I'd come. If I felt sorry about not finding a replacement milk cow, I don't remember it.

At twilight I found a measure of peace in Ed's steady gait, and I stopped spitting blood about the time we crossed the gentle flow of the Niobrara at Morris's Bridge. I strained my grit-laden eyes for any sign of life there, a place where Albert and me and the others had run so carefree and wild, a place inhabited by specters of a different time.

What dark demon had so possessed Kid Wade as to come home and fire up the old funeral pyres?

Because that's what was coming, even if he couldn't see it.

Funeral pyres.

This time around, I was determined to be on the right side of things.

"Owww, oh, oh, oh —" I grit my teeth against the anguish of Trudy's washcloth as she cleaned my cuts and gashes.

"Calm down," Trudy said, "I didn't even touch you."

"You did, so. Damned if I didn't feel your pitchfork twixt my ribs."

She dropped the rag into a white granite pan of fresh boiled water, saying, "Do it yourself."

"That's no way to be."

"You want to court a fever for a week, be my guest. I'd rather see you on the mend."

"Aw, heck."

The look on Trudy's face — like a schoolmarm with my chalkboard spelling. I picked up the washcloth, squeezed the water out, and patted my side just over the third rib. "Owtch."

"Let me inspect your work when you're done."

Trudy had me outside the house and stripped to the waist, the indigo night sky sprinkled with glittering white powder stars. Along with my hurts, the immensity of night made me feel small and insignificant.

Cramped and miserable, I dabbed at the sore, dark, puffy splotch on my side and the torn seams of my hide.

My skull felt like a pumpkin patch gourd, knobby and hard, and Trudy said it looked to be the same shades of orange, white, and green.

Even so, she had the faith of Job that I would heal. Me, I was the doubting Thomas.

"I think I'm done."

After she carried a fresh pan of steaming salted water out from the house to the stool where I sat, she said, "Just so you know, Wade hasn't been back." She squeezed out a fresh rag, handed it over. "He got what he wanted. He knows where you stand. I doubt he'll be back."

The Winchester was on the ground beside my stocking feet.

Trudy's Greener shotgun leaned up against the door.

We were ready for him if he came.

Just in case she was wrong.

"I was wrong to go it alone," I said.

"I knew that before you left." She ran a gentle hand along the back of my head, resting her fingers on my neck. "But I love you for trying."

"It was a durn fool move."

"At least you learned something. You won't do it again."

"Next time I'll have help. Next time he won't hold all the cards."

"Or, we could avoid a next time. We could leave the entire thing alone."

I told her about Cap Burnham and Manke and Ted Roberts. I told her about the stolen sorrels and the meeting at Manke's house the next Saturday.

"Leave it alone, Gus. It's a problem for the community to handle."

"We belong to the community," I said.

"We belong to ourselves."

"Look where that got us — short one cow and me getting ambushed."

"Joining up with a group of vigs won't make things any better, Gus."

"We need to band together to protect ourselves. Protect our families."

Trudy brushed a lock of hair from my forehead and soothed my bruised cheekbones with her fingertips. "Protect ourselves? Like Otto Randolph and the vigs who hanged our friends? The only excuse they had for their bloody shenanigans was that they were protecting themselves. You know what happened to them, they —"

I reached up and put a forefinger against her lips. "We promised not to talk about it."

"Say it, Gus. What happened to them. Say it."

I held my jaw stiff, but I said it. "We killed them."

"And we buried them behind the house."

Regarding Randolph's fate, the two of us were sworn to secrecy. The kind of secret we would take to our own graves.

"Is that how you want to end up?" she said.

Worm food, I thought. Plunked down and covered over someplace, fertilizer for taters and carrots and wildflowers in a garden. They were more useful in death than they ever had been in life.

"The difference is," I tried to explain, "Randolph's bunch was impulsive. They had no rules to go by. They just went willy-nilly after any poor dumb cowpoke with a mope on his face."

"How come you're so sure this time will be different?"

"Ted Roberts said so. He said these men are *organized*. That means a written agreement. Bylaws. A constitution." At least I hoped that's what it meant. I was spinning blankets of caterpillar fuzz.

Trudy's expression showed skepticism, so I kept at it. "It's only for a short time. I promise. Until the county puts law officers in place, we're all of us law-abiding citizens at the mercy of people like John and Albert. It won't be more than a month or two."

"A lot can happen in a month or two."

I agreed with her on that much, and I told her so.

"A lot of men can lose their livelihood. Look where we are now, with no Betty, no milk. Thank goodness we don't have a little one."

Just like that, she turned away fast and I kicked myself for running off at the mouth again, not thinking, just spilling my guts. Now I'd hurt her because she blamed herself for us not having kids, and that's the one thing she wanted more than anything else in the whole entire world.

Raising her eyes to the sky, she pulled her sweater close and wrapped her arms around herself in a rocking hug.

Dammit. My heart hurt for her — and for us — all over again.

Not because of John Wade or the Pony Boys but for our lonesome nights after Sonny went to the barn and only ourselves to chatter at. I hurt because we talked about horse mange or rabbits in the garden or all the magnificent repairs I'd do to the barn if only I ever got down to Long Pine to pick up a load of wood.

But we didn't have what she wanted most.

I had the glorious timber now, but it didn't fill the hole inside or the growing space between me and Trudy.

I swear, I clutched onto the holy opportunity of joining up with those boys with both hands. The Word of God was in the news about Cap Burnham's group, and Ted Roberts was my prophet.

I was ready to do anything to stem the

onrush of solitude we both felt settling between us. Trudy sat with a thumb tucked in her cheerless Bible, and I fell asleep in my chair. Every night before climbing between the sheets, we made sure to do our duty, just in case this time something might spark in the ever-widening expanse.

"This is what we need to do," I said, firm, the way a man should talk to his wife, expecting her to follow. "Tomorrow, I'll get Sonny to help me put a bar across the inside of the door. We'll take the iron hinges off a couple stable gates from the barn and make board shutters for the windows."

"It sounds like you're outfitting a fort."

"And why not? Didn't the Army put Fort Niobrara up when the Sioux got testy? It's what men do when they're threatened. They fortify themselves. They set up boundaries."

"You were talking about community. It sounds to me like you're fixing to build an army and everybody's a soldier."

"I'm done talking about it, Trudy."

At this point, she was being pigheaded, trying to open things up again.

At least arguing kept my mind off my aches and pains.

Either way, I'd made my decision.

"What about Albert?" she said. This time she went for my heart, and it almost worked, except that I'd already been chewing things over during my entire miserable ride home from the cow pond.

I shrugged, and the pain between my shoulders felt like a knife. "Albert's another one who needs to know he's not welcome here," I said.

"What if you find out he's personally responsible for Manke and Richardson's sorrels? What if he took them? Are you willing to string him up, Gus?"

I knew she would ask.

"I think it was Tony Pike or Willy Ransom who done the deed. And we know John Wade stole our Betty."

But I was just saying it. I knew Kid Wade was likely behind it all.

Trudy knew that I knew.

Determined, she tried again, "What if you boys catch Albert directly with a stolen horse? Will you forget your past friendship?"

"It's not like you to kick me when I'm down."

"It's a fair question."

I answered out of anger. Or pain. Or a combination of both with annoyance. "If we catch Kid Wade, I'll lift that bastard up by the neck as high as the moon."

I was overexcited and hurt and scared. But right then, I meant ever word.

Trudy's gaze went through me like I wasn't even there. Or like she didn't recognize me.

But once down that road, there was no turning back. I knew it in my heart and mind, both. Sonny and me would nail things down in Pleasant Valley, and come Saturday, I'd ride to Virgil Manke's house and sell my soul over the counter.

But that ain't right, either. I didn't think of it so much as selling my soul. Only leasing it for a little while.

And — oh, my God — for the next few weeks, wasn't it fun being a vig?

CHAPTER SIX

The Niobrara Mutual Protective Association wasn't restricted to horse thieves and cattle rustlers. It wasn't explicitly stated in the bylaws, but we took it upon ourselves to bust evil wherever we found it, like King Arthur and his knights — but American, like the Union Army with carbines and endless wells of sincerity.

I pledged myself, under oath, to the Association down at Virgil Manke's house, the last week of October, sitting beside Ted Roberts at a walnut dinner table opposite Cap Burnham. We sipped a bitter English tea our host insisted was good for rheumatism, and I signed my name to a long piece of business along with seventeen other men. We used a feather pen to put down the ink, a quill Manke said some Union general used twenty years before to sign a treaty with the Brúle Sioux.

Out on the prairie, I'd never been inside

such a fancy house as Manke's, slathered in pink and green floral wallpaper and trimmed with polished walnut. And here we were, a mangy arrangement of boar dogs and bull pups, with our brushed felt hats and handy sidearms. Not a man jack among us was unarmed. There were long guns on hooks above three doors, and Cap brought his Sharps Big Fifty just for show.

Cap was the kind of man who gave you a nod and you felt like the whole world was offering its hand. He was plainspoken and handsome with a heavy combed mustache the color of deep plowed loam, and the lines on his face were put there by years of laughter.

He wasn't the most wealthy man around, but he was the best of us, a cow man and an attorney, and everything about him, from his stamped leather suspenders to his trimmed fingernails, made you want to be a better person through the virtues of reason, discipline, and community. I still believe that about Cap Burnham to this day and will lick the man who says otherwise.

As soon as we signed our names to the agreement Cap had drawn up, we were outside in our saddles.

"When dealing with devils, cast a wide

loop, boys. We'll sort out the details later." Cap Burnham held that gloved hand high in the noontime sun, and when it dropped, we bolted away like Satan himself breathed fire at our heels. Maybe he did.

"Yeee-ha!"

I spurred Ed into line behind Ted Roberts's paint and flew away toward Bassett, cyclone lightning with a frigid, crisp wind at my ears.

We fell in alongside Cap Burnham and Virgil Manke on the trail, me bareheaded, my hair going every which way, and Ted in his beaver skin top hat. We found the Barlow Boys soon enough, a pair of heartless skunks who'd been tricking the folks all along the railroad with a game involving a cast-iron bank safe.

Cast a wide loop, Cap said, and he meant it.

Over yellow dried bunchgrass, Ted and I rode into a clearing on the low side of the canyon between Cap and Virgil Manke, and wouldn't you know, it was the same grassy damn meadow with the algae-covered cow pond where John Wade pounded the daylights out of me.

The difference today — there was a crowd of nearly two-dozen people gathered like a coffee and pie social, except nobody was

83

wearing their Sunday duds. Around two dozen good folks, and children too, circled the pond on three sides, up to their ankles in cow-chewed grass. A lady I found out later was Biff Barlow's second cousin sold lemonade and cold coffee under one of the three leafless cottonwood trees, and another Barlow cousin sat on the bench of a big wagon nearby.

Biff was a brawny man with a smooth baby face and neatly combed red hair under a round bowler hat. He had plump cheeks and big, square ears like horse blinders. His brother, Clem, stood a few inches from the bank, knee-deep in pond scum, his trousers bunched up at the knee caps. He looked like a scrawny version of Biff, only with no cap and a dusting of beard, and he held a length of rope loose in his withered hands. The rope led off into the middle of the pond.

Easy as you please, like he was at a family reunion, Cap rode his big buckskin right up to the chattering crowd, calling out, "Biff Barlow? Where are you, Biff?"

A couple sodbusters stepped aside so Biff could walk a little farther out from the pond and talk to us.

"Who's that calling my name?" With ears

like that, he couldn't help but hear the summons.

There are criminals cool as a turnip cellar and others with nerves like wet noodles; both ways can have an advantage. The nonplussed man can weather a storm and hold to his trickery under the worst kind of duress. The anxious fellow is forever on guard and can often see trouble coming before his counterpart.

Biff was neither cool and competent, nor especially wary. His was exactly the wrong personality for misconduct.

He was, at heart, an innocent.

But I had yet to learn it, so I kept my attention fixed on the six-gun secured with a button to his belt and tied at the knee.

Nobody in this good crowd of Christians was looking to go to heaven tonight. I wanted to keep it that way.

My carbine stayed out, flat across my lap.

If Biff went for his sidearm, I'd blow his guts out.

No joke, I used to think tough thoughts like that to myself all the time, especially when I rode with Cap.

Again, Biff said, "Who's that?"

"I'm Cap Burnham. My friend is John Augustus."

Biff tapped his forehead. "Burnham . . .

Burnham. Never heard of you."

"I've got a few cows, yes, sir."

"You're also one of the Niobrara regulators they tell about."

"What folks tell about doesn't interest me. What does interest me, is what you and your brother are doing here today." Cap glanced over at me, and I took the lead.

"How about you explain yourselves, Biff?" I indicated the clumps of men and women, the kids leaping and running in the grass, the lady selling lemonade. "What's this family affair all about?"

But, of course, I already knew. Cap had filled us in on the way over.

Resting on the bottom of the pond at the end of Clem Barlow's hemp line was a cast-iron safe. What the brothers did was scout out a body of water a day or so ahead of time, drop the safe to the bottom, then come into a town pretending to have discovered the remnants of a robbery. Then they gathered a crowd of gullible folks and auctioned off the safe with its unknown amount of treasure.

I asked Cap, "What happens when they open the safe and find out there's nothing inside?"

"Like any gamble, it's just too bad for the sucker who loses."

"I don't like 'em tricking people," I said.

"We don't either, Gus."

So we set out to put a stop to it.

Biff took my request as an opportunity to give his spiel.

"We're the Barlow Brothers. I'm Biff, and this is my brother, Clem." Clem held up the rope and a few people clapped.

Biff continued his performance. "We Barlows make our money recovering artifacts of a bygone day. With shovel, rake, or rope, we're here to use the God-given might of brain and brawn to deliver treasure into your hands and joy to your heart." To emphasize his sincerity, he doffed his topper and clutched the hat to his chest. "We make only as much money as you care to pay. Taking our chances right alongside the good people we serve, you'll find our expeditions and excavations are not only fair and legal, but entertaining to behold."

While Biff rattled on, Cap told Manke and Ted, "You two circle around the men at the pond." To me, he said, "You just play along with whatever I say."

"You think they'll try and give us the slip?" I said.

Cap stroked his chin, stuck out his lip. "Naw. They won't leave their safe behind. And from the looks of things, it's underwater now. There's money to be made, they'll stick around." He gave me a wink. "We got 'em, Gus."

He said it straight, man to man, and he was talking to me like he might've been talking to Frymire or C.C. Dodge.

Like I wasn't some snot-nosed ex-outlaw, but one of them — a man working with 'em.

Doing my fair share.

Biff spread out his arms, then dropped them to the sides of his corpulent frame. Obviously a boy who never missed a meal, I saw his belt was on its very last hole, barely reaching the buckle.

"Now you all know who we are and what we're doing."

"Seems to me you could find a better line of work," I told him.

"We get by, I guess." When he answered, I watched for a telltale twitch of the plump fingers nearest his gun. "You interested in bidding on the treasure we've latched on to?"

"How about you tell us about it?" Cap said.

Ted and Manke had assumed positions at two o'clock and ten o'clock on the opposite banks of the water, and Cap nodded to them before addressing me with a low voice so nobody else could hear. "These pretenders have been pulling this trick all the way downriver to the Missouri."

At the pond, Biff raised his voice. "We're all fortunate today, ladies and gentlemen, to be privy to the hard work and brilliance of my brother, Clem, a man whose keen skills at manhunting and trailblazing have come together to benefit all of us."

From his spot on the bank of a pond, a young man in a flat-brimmed straw hat cupped his hand near his mouth. "Get on with it."

Biff chuckled. "Here's a fellow nearly as excited as I am."

Another man shouted his query. "Is it gold? Silver? How much did Clem find?"

Biff patted down the air, indicating a need for patience. "As I said, Clem's a man-hunter. He's been following the infamous Stone Deacon gang for more than a year. Maybe you've heard of them?"

I had not. From the look on his face, neither had Cap Burnham.

Biff said, "The Deacons absconded with a safe from a prominent Dakota Territory bank more than ten years ago. Reportedly full of Union stamped gold bricks, the safe was loaded onto a wagon and driven with haste south into Nebraskaland."

"Let me guess," Cap said, "with a United

States Marshal dogging their escape."

"Precisely right," Biff said. "This man's heard the tale." Several of the women turned to nod at Cap with admiration, and a couple men tipped their hat.

"You played right into Biff Barlow's hand," I said.

"As a certified attorney, I guess I've seen just about everything and heard about it twice. Watch and learn, son. Watch and learn."

Biff finished his mythical yarn. "The trail was too hot, and the Deacons needed to drop their contraband somewhere where it could be retrieved later. After an exhausting few months of inquiry and exploration — and no small expense in financial handouts to some mighty scurvy ruffians — my brother learned that the safe was right here, under the water of this humble Carns cow pond."

I asked Cap, "How many times do you suppose the Barlow Brothers have drowned this particular safe?"

"Enough to grow mold on the hinges."

The same man with the straw hat asked, "How much gold is inside?" and I decided right then he was a shill, working the crowd on behalf of the brothers.

Somebody said, "Tell us what the contents

of the safe are worth."

"That's where you come in," Biff announced to the crowd. "We have no more idea than you do how much the safe holds. What we're going to do is open up the bidding at five dollars. The first man or woman to pledge that much will be entitled to whatever is inside the safe once Clem and some of you burly men from the crowd haul her up." And here he paused for effect and a conniving, wry smile. "Unless, of course, somebody bids higher."

Biff put his head on a fast swivel. "Who's the first to offer five dollars?"

"Here," said the shill.

"I'll pay ten," came a second bid.

Biff said, "Ten, do I hear twelve?"

Cap raised his hand. "Fifteen!"

"Thank you, sir."

I bent low and Cap followed suit as I whispered. "How high you think the bid will go?"

Cap glanced up at the clear blue sky. "Judging by the pleasant weather and stink of human greed? I'd wager it'll break $100."

"How do we stop 'em?"

"Play along with me." Cap winked. "Like I said, watch and learn."

Next thing you know, it was Cap giving a spiel.

"Let's define our terms once more," Cap said, interrupting Biff's auction yodel. "You located the safe. You tied a rope around it. But you have no idea how much is inside."

"Correct."

"You've never seen the safe before today?"

"Never."

Cap addressed the crowd, pointing at the heavy duty buckboard wagon and pair of Percheron work horses fixed to it. "You promise you didn't haul that safe in and drop it in the water earlier today?"

Some of the men shifted back and forth from one foot to another. It was clear they hadn't paid any attention to the wagon. Or if they had, they didn't think much about it.

Biff Barlow managed an expression of pure disgust at the accusation. "No, sir — we most certainly did not." I kept my eye on the hand closest to his holster.

Cap smiled. "If the safe was underwater when you all got here, who went down and tied the rope around it?"

"I did," Clem said.

"How come your clothes aren't wet?"

This time more men showed their discomfort and Biff's face went from white to red. "Are you calling me a liar, friend?"

"First off, I ain't your friend. Secondly, yes. You're right. I'm calling you a liar."

Biff flung out his arm. "There's likely to be hundreds of dollars in gold inside that safe."

"I'll tell you what," Cap said, removing a piece of paper and stub pencil from his shirt pocket. "I'm going to give this slip of paper to that man over there." He pointed at Ted Roberts. "Then you finish the auction and haul up the safe."

Cap did as he promised, but when Ted took possession of the slip of paper, Biff hesitated.

"What's a matter?" Cap said. "Yank 'er up outta there."

"What was on the slip of paper?"

"You really want to know?"

"I surely do want to know."

Cap raised his voice so everybody could hear. "I wrote down the serial number that's carved into the back of the safe. I got it from a man who attended this same show the last time the Barlow Brothers discovered a drowned safe." He shrugged. "I guess if this is a different safe from last time, the numbers won't match."

Clem dropped the rope. The lemonade lady started to fold up her stand.

Biff's face went from pink to red. His fingers brushed the butt of his gun.

I jerked up my rifle, put my cheek on the

stock and the bead over Biff's heart. "You be still, Mr. Barlow."

Biff tossed his arms into the sky. "Don't shoot."

The crowd laughed with nervous tension. Then one of the men demanded. "Haul up the safe, Barlow. C'mon, haul 'er up."

Another man said, "Haul 'er up."

Then another. And a fourth.

"Haul 'er up."

"Haul 'er up."

Cap swung his arms around like the conductor of a church choir, and I joined in as the entire crowd took up the chant. "Haul 'er up. Haul 'er up!" We had the whole bunch going, surrounding the Barlow brothers on all sides.

When Clem tried to climb out of the water, leaving the rope behind, somebody pelted him with a ball of mud. Next came a shoe. Then a little kid slapped him with a hat.

Finally, Clem fell backwards in a tremendous splash and a barrage of laughter, and everybody knew right then the thing was a trick.

The four of us regulators kept our guns out and pointed, and you've never seen two old boys pack up their gear and haul ass away up the road like them Barlow Boys.

Lots of men slapped us on the back and came to shake our hands, and we got invited over to four or five houses for coffee and pie. Being the sociable gents we were, we accepted with hearts full of humility.

By the end of the day, my middle bloated up like a calf on alfalfa hay.

Everybody forgot the iron safe, and I figure it's still under that pond to this day.

Later on, Ted Roberts showed me the piece of paper Cap gave him, and don't you know there wasn't a durn thing written on it. No serial number at all.

It was clean and white as the new fallen snow.

These were the kinds of good deeds we did for the citizens of the Niobrara country, and nothing or nobody can ever make me ashamed of those times and those men who proved themselves to be my friends. Although, to be honest, some of them proved not to be my friends, and all of them are long dead now, some shotgunned in two or hanged from a whistling post.

But don't you know the four of us celebrated our rout of the Barlow Boys that night at the end of October — singing and hollering all the way back home.

Chapter Seven

A week later, Cap had a lead on Tony Pike, a towheaded runt who'd soured a Manke deal on an Arabian racehorse by thieving the thoroughbred from the seller before Virgil could lay eyes on it. Cap hoped a raid on Pike's sorry shack at Eagle Creek would lead us to Kid Wade.

Then Albert would take us to Manke and Richardson's six missing sorrels.

Somewhere in the mix, I'd find the Kid's dad and get my own revenge on him.

"It's like your mama's embroidery hoop," Cap said. "One stitch leads to the next. Or maybe a better comparison was the time my sweater got hooked on a piece of newly made barbed-wire fence, what they called the thorny fence, or *devil's rope.* I got spurred and didn't notice and by the time I'd walked twenty feet, half my sleeve trailed out behind, all unraveled. If we can get Pike on the hook, we'll be one step closer to undoing Kid Wade's gang."

I remembered Tony as a booger-picking sprout, no younger than Ted Roberts, but I'll wager running with Albert made him feel almighty old and wizened beyond the green in his limbs.

By that November of 1883, the newspapers were fawning all over Al, calling him *captain* of the miscreants. Like he'd earned their respect. The papers were always fickle like that. Pounding the drum when we regulators won a skirmish. Equally gleeful when we lost.

They built Kid Wade into a legend and referred to his friends as a "desperate gang of cutthroats."

Hell, in all the time I'd run with Albert, I never once thought of him as desperate. The papers picked up the Kid moniker and sometimes, Slippery Jack. They made a fortune bragging no rope could ring him in, no prison could hold him. Albert used the name Slippery Jack himself, along with Sam Gordon.

Funny how I had always thought of him as my pal.

Eventually, I learned different, of course.

I recognized Albert Wade and his kind for what they were — selfish ruffians who couldn't grow up. Any one of them would sell you down the river to save their own dirty hides, and they'd do it with a smile on their face. Somebody needed to bring them into line, and I decided to act like a man and volunteer.

Racing my buckskin fast around a cedar grove on the way to Pike's place, I caught up with Ted Roberts, and he reined in beside me to point out where Cap Burnham and Manke had disappeared down a steep gully trail at Eagle Creek.

"Ol' Stinky Pike is quick as a fart in a windstorm, but I think we got him this time, August John. His shack is just below the ridge."

"You reckon he's hiding out, the way Cap says?"

"Only one way to find out." Ted carried an Army Peacemaker that was too big for his paw, and he always tipped to port when he pulled it from his belt holster. "Let's go down and roust him."

Ted was thrilled to be a part of something big and far beyond what he'd ever expected of his life, building a community without ever having learned to build as much as a birdhouse. Ted couldn't put together a fence or fix a saddle cinch or a wagon hub, but he imagined he could fix problems between men. He assumed a quick finger on a hot trigger could solve anything.

Riding with us regulators, he'd shared some glory and hoped to get a girl and thought maybe he'd become a big man in somebody's eyes.

I believed it then, too.

I don't think so now.

But what a jolt of excitement I felt as I jerked the Winchester from Ed's saddle boot, picturing Pike down there huddled up and scared inside his shack on the banks of Eagle Creek. Probably the bastard was shaking in his undershorts.

We weren't planning to hang him.

Despite what some people said, we weren't some kind of lawless lynch mob.

Cap wasn't about hurting anybody — he was about getting justice for Virgil Manke and Henry Richardson and the citizens of Brown County.

Just letting Tony know we were after him would bring him back to the straight and narrow road.

The same couldn't be said for John Wade. Him, I wanted to sock good for the drubbing he gave me. And then I'd do worse again.

His case was different.

And going cold.

It was the first of November, and I was

more than a little bit impatient.

"You think Tony will lead us to the Wades?" I said.

"Maybe," Ted answered. He rode on ahead and dropped down into the ravine behind the others.

Maybe wasn't good enough.

Before following along, I pulled a tin flask from my vest pocket and coated my throat with some spiced rum.

The booze smoothed me out, and I thanked God and Sonny Clausen for teaching me the fine art of gentlemanly sipping. But really, I did more drinking with Ted Roberts than I ever did with Sonny.

With my rifle in hand, I was invincible.

"I'm coming for you, Tony Pike," I said. At the same time, a spry metallic warning clicked into my ears.

The sound of a gun hammer, settling into place.

A voice followed along, and he wasn't bashful. "Seems to me, you've got it all ass-backwards, August John."

I was sober enough not to try something stupid. But no man gripping a rifle dared turn and fire on a cocked pistol in his back. Add to it that Tony Pike was a dead-on shot.

I said, "How you doing, Tony?" He stood in the underbrush directly behind me.

"How long have you been hiding there under the maple leaves?"

"How 'bout call me *Sam Gordon*?"

"Oh, Jesus — not you too."

"Get down off that shavetail and face me like a man."

"You and me got nothing to talk about . . . Sam."

"Get on down, anyhow."

"You want my horse?"

"Maybe I do, Gus. So how about you oblige me before I launch your brains up to the moon?"

"You always were eager to pull a trigger," I said. "But you wouldn't get too far. My friends are just down over the ridge. They'll hear the shot and come charging down on you like Jesus on a Sunday morning whore."

Tony still had the same laugh he always had.

"What's funny?" I said.

He chuckled again. "You talking about those whores. I heard that's what you are these days, Gus. I heard you're a whore for the Niobrara regulators."

"By God, I won't take that kind of talk. Not even from you." I had yet to turn around, yet to drop my rifle. I wondered if maybe I had a chance of nicking him.

Tony said, "I hear tell you take a lot of

guff off Cap and Virgil Manke's boys. Albert's heard it too."

"What do you know about Albert? Where is he?"

"He's around."

"Tell him I want to see him. I want to talk to him about his old man."

"You can suck wind, Gus."

I caught the shadow of movement out of the corner of my eye and held up my left arm to ward off the impact. But Tony was too quick. I'd been so concerned about a bullet, I hadn't considered a tree limb to my shoulder.

Tony always had a good arm, whether roping or roughhousing, and now I was a recipient of the latter, falling sideways, twisting so I'd land on my butt and not my head, trying hard to keep hold of my Winchester. Failing on both accounts.

Slamming into the ground, I lost my breath along with my gun, and Tony was already in Ed's saddle before I could move.

I climbed to my feet only to watch him ride in the opposite direction of the valley, my buckskin galloping away into the distance. I rubbed my sore noggin.

The rotten skunk got away clean.

While retrieving my rifle, I caught the smell of burning wood in the air, then watched a tower of gray smoke angle up from the gorge below. I carried the Winchester to the lip of the trail. Down below, Virgil Manke was darting around the base of a ramshackle hut, setting a torch to each corner of the place.

Arson was a hobby of his, and he fired things more and more, the longer we continued the hunt. "It's not only practical, driving these animals from their homes," he said, "it sends a message."

I triggered my rifle three times in the air. Once to get Cap's and Ted's and Virgil Manke's attention.

Twice out of mad frustration.

"You ain't always gonna win the first time around," Sonny Clausen said the following evening, lifting his jug and tipping back his chin like a thirsty turkey to let the rum slide down his gullet. He handed over the crock, letting me take a drink. I handed it back, and Sonny finished it off. "These Pony Boys are crafty."

"Don't call 'em that," I said. "Don't ever call 'em that."

"What? *Pony Boys?* Ain't they —"

"No, they ain't. There haven't been any Pony Boys since the day Llewellyn took Doc off to jail. There won't ever be any again.

It's what they called *us,* but it's not what we're calling *them.*"

"The newspapers says they're Pony Boys. That's what I'll call 'em."

"The newspapers can go to hell."

I'd been working up a simmering boil since losing Ed to Tony Pike the day before when Ted Roberts gave me a ride home on his mule.

If Sonny wanted to share his liquor with me, that was fine. If he wanted to visit a bit, that suited me okay. But be damned if I'd sit in my own barn and let the old bag of wind insult me. I looked around the barn for a second jug and found it under Sonny's bedroll.

Betty's cow pen smelled of horse sweat and dry cow flop, pigeons and musty hay. It smelled empty.

I jerked the cork out of Sonny's crock and took a long drink.

Sonny said, "You boys all used to be so close. You and the Beltezores and Eph Weatherwax. You and Albert." He clucked his tongue. "I'm not ashamed to say you used to scare Jesus out of me."

"Albert's changed since those days, Sonny. Maybe he's hooked up with his old man. Or maybe it was the jail time in Anamosa. Either way, he's not like he used to be, and . . . shucks, he damn well should've grown out of all this nonsense by now."

"Riding around with a bunch of men on horseback?"

"Exactly."

"Hootin' and hollering, always on the hunt?"

"Yep. That's exactly what I mean."

"Sounds a lot like you regulators."

"You're determined to pester me tonight, aren't you, old man?"

"I just think you might stay home more."

"Hell, Trudy's saying the same damn thing."

"Maybe you should listen to her."

I couldn't help but laugh, this pee-soaked old possum who'd never been married or had a steady girl telling me how to run my home. Fine! Well, it irked me like thunder. I wondered if he was trying to act like a father to some kid he never had, or maybe he thought he was being a pal to Trudy.

I put the jug down hard, too hard, and cracked it in half. All the rum leaked out between us, but I was downhill enough most of it soaked into my pants. I jumped up and danced around — Ridiculous! — but I wasn't in a mood to laugh.

Amber light in the sky caught my attention.

"Waxing gibbous," I said. "Another few days, we'll have a full moon."

Sonny pulled himself up and waddled to the open door. "Huh. What do you know about that?"

I brushed at my pants, then strode back to big Levi and tossed a saddle on his back.

Sonny followed, bashful like I might knock his block off.

"You're not going back out?" he said.

"Why wouldn't I? Clear night, enough bright moon to light my way. Cap wants us running night patrols over our territories."

"What we were just talking about. Did you hear what I was saying?"

I pulled Levi's cinch tight. "I surely did. Did you hear me?"

"What should I tell Trudy?"

I threw myself onto the big gelding's back, unsure, but frankly unconcerned.

"Suppose I bring Ed or Betty home with me," I said. "You don't think Trudy will be glad of that?" It sounded like such a good idea, I made it into a plan. "You tell Trudy, I'm bringing home what is rightfully ours. You tell her I'm going out there to make things right."

Of course, that's when things started to go wrong.

If only I could've seen it.

106

But how could I? Telling the past is a heck of a lot easier than telling the future.

I bumbled around the country all night long, followed a hunch to visit Holt Creek where Doc once had a lean-to set up between two old cottonwoods next to a roughhewn corral with a makeshift cattle race. Right there, I stumbled over Tony Pike, complete with a pen full of stolen sorrels, and I delivered them at gunpoint to Cap Burnham at Carns.

Just like Cap said, one by one, the ring was coming undone.

Nobody could stop us.

Only God could stop us.

CHAPTER EIGHT

The Ledger is pleased to note the fact of the entire breaking up by the vigilants of the notorious and desperate gang of horse thieves, whose depredations have been so numerous the past year in north Nebraska and southern Dakota from the eastern portions of both to the Black Hills, as to greatly deter newcomers from bringing anything but the poorest stock and aiding in the retarding of immigration to this section more than any one thing else. In fact, so unsafe has it been to bring good horses into the country that settlers here would warn their friends in the east, who contemplated locating, to bring nothing with them but "plugs"; and as a consequence the resources of one of the best portions of the Union have not been developed to one half the extent they would have been had a different state of affairs existed.

The Stuart Ledger, by way of the *Holt County Banner,* November 1883

"C'mon around there, August John, rope that colt before she skitters away."

Cap Burnham's glove made a high circle in the early morning moonlight, as I worked the reins. Ed's hooves kicked up the range clay in a tremendous about-face.

"Waa-hooo!" We fell away to the left, circling out from the other regulators, angling our way around the booming half-dozen sorrels, my arm thrown up in a heroic pose, my lasso, comfortable and twirling in a firm hand.

I'd been up all night driving those missing sorrels to Virgil Manke's place with Tony and Cap, but it still felt good to once again be in the saddle, *my saddle,* on board my buckskin pal. Ed must have felt the same way, because he ran and maneuvered like a kid free from school, his blue-breath pulsing out in quicksilver clouds.

"That a'way, Gus." Ted Roberts flashed into the corner of my eye, yipping and hollering his encouragement. "We got 'em on the run."

I pitched my lasso, dead-on, and snared

that little mare like she was nailed to the sod.

Ted rolled off his black charger to take control of the colt, and I pounded on past, up the raggedy-weed-covered knoll of frozen bluestem where Cap sat in the saddle of a big gray gelding. Virgil Manke was on a dun mare beside him. "Nice work, kid." You could see his smile of approval under that glowing white mustache all the way to where Long Pine sat in the distance.

"Thanks."

Between them, Tony Pike sat moping on a swayback mount, his hands in his lap, his wrists forced together with a hemp bow tie. "You always had a way with livestock, Gus."

Manke agreed. "You need to take on Frymire at the next county shindig."

"Frymire's the best man there is with a rope," I said.

"I wouldn't count on it," Cap said. "I think you're better."

"Yip, yip, yip!" Another cry came from below, and the four of us turned our horses to watch Ben Frymire and Myron Berry make the final drive, stuffing the galloping bunch of six recovered sorrels, along with a bonus mare and gelding, between two deep planted pine gate poles into a snug wood corral.

The ground thrummed with the whirling, whinnying mass of chestnut horseflesh. My blood thrilled to watch them scuffle and gallop, a blend of starlit white dust and tossed flowing manes, tails riding high and teeth bared in the indigo night. "There's nothing like 'em on the face of the earth."

"And there never will be," Manke said.

He was a horse man through and through. It was his life's passion.

"I've got some money squirreled away in a jar back home," Tony said. "We might make a deal if you'd free my hands up."

"I'll say this for your pal, Gus. He's got a sense of humor."

Tony's bony head turned slow on his stalk of a neck to look at me. "That's right, Gus. I'm your pal, ain't I?"

I told Manke, "Tony's another one of these donkeys who calls himself Sam Gordon. No matter how many times we meet, Sam Gordon ain't no friend of mine." I said it with a sneer, but it didn't get the rise I'd hoped for out of Tony. Instead of complaining, he just sat there staring at me like it was me who was hooked up with a different name.

Like it was me who was the stranger.

Frymire hauled the reluctant gate shut behind the last racer and draped his elbows back over the top rail to wait for Ted Roberts.

Manke was in great humor, having his stolen animals once again secure in his tight prairie pen, and a horse thief prisoner t'boot.

Cap said, "You're awful chipper for a dour old cuss who dresses in heavy gray all the time."

Manke answered. "Ain't Henry Richardson gonna be pleased?"

I felt pretty cheerful myself, whistling "Yellow Easter Bonnets" at Ted as he shuffled past to put the colt in with his mama.

"Let's us adjourn to the house and break out some drinkin' stuff. We'll have a celebration," Manke said.

"Sounds about right," Cap Burnham said. "What about it, Gus? You got time to pull a jug?"

"I reckon I'd tip a glass," I said, "once we get this bunch settled in."

"You leave Frymire and Myron to do that," Manke said. "Those two fellows wouldn't know a drink if you spilled it on their lap."

"Methodists," Burnham said. "Nothing against 'em, you understand. They just have some odd beliefs."

I remembered the church social at Bassett. "I understand they fry up some fine chicken," I said.

Burnham roared with laughter, and I even got another grin out of Manke. "That they do, indeed, son. They do, indeed."

Tony said, "What about me? Do I get a drink?"

"Probably not," Burnham said.

Down the hill we went, me riding between two of the biggest men in Holt and Brown County combined, prodding a horse thief along ahead of me. Manke led the way toward his house.

Cap Burnham led me and Tony through the kitchen after penning up them sorrel horses. The place smelled of that bitter-sweet tea and lemon oil. Manke met us in the dining room.

"It's lucky Gus stumbled across your hidey-hole," he said. "I guess your secret pen wasn't so secret, Tony."

"It's a new one on me too, boys," I said — maybe too quick because Burnham raised an eyebrow, then glanced at his partner.

Nobody said anything more until the three of us were bellied up to the same table we'd shared before with the other vigilantes, and Tony Pike sat alone across from us, still trussed up tight, the wild pink and green

113

wallpaper flickering sort of moldy blue in the morning kerosene firelight.

He was dressed as I'd seen him earlier that week. His eggshell white shirt had a ruffle, and buttons punched out of mussel shells like they made in Missouri. He wore a round beige cap that Ted Roberts knocked off when he came in and plopped down in the chair next to me.

Tony's eyes burned fierce with hate. He was three or four years older than Ted and naturally still looked at him like a kid. But Ted had grown taller than either Tony or me. Not a one of us was a kid anymore.

"Ain't polite to wear a hat inside," Ted said. "Especially at the table."

I noticed Ted kept his top hat in place.

Cap said, "Where's the others?"

"Frymire and Myron had to scoot," Ted said. "I'll take a shot of whatever you're drinking."

Manke picked up a brown bottle from the floor and handed it to him. "You'll find a glass over on the sideboard."

"I hate for those boys to not be here," Cap said.

"Me too," Manke said, but I don't think he meant it. The look on his face said he was just as glad to deal out justice with as few onlookers as possible. If Cap and me

114

and Ted had wanted to go, Manke would've been first up to hold open the door.

But he needed us here if we were going to go by the rules.

Before the Association's constitution got passed around for official signatures, Cap Burnham had read the bylaws — like any of us would remember them, but we were expected to eventually. Cap had things written in there like Clause 6, Part B, reading "such and such should never go do this or that thing," but mostly it was to keep us on the straight and narrow, which we all knew, and pledged allegiance to.

No one of us alone had the right to pass judgment on anybody. A minimum of four men was required during an interview, and we were all supposed to stick up for each other.

I mean, I didn't hear or see anything that wasn't straight up moral and ethical.

Now it was the four of us, and Cap leaned back in his chair with a heavy sigh.

"Let's talk about what comes next with these horses," and he meant not only Ed and the half-dozen sorrels that we just got back, but I had learned there were more ponies up and gone missing, including Ben Frymire's Shady Jane.

Manke sat at Burnham's right hand, his

white hair looking beige in the shadows, taking ten years from his face. "Frymire reports they got away with Shady Jane, her harness, fancy six-string saddle, blanket . . . everything."

"How's Miss Baghdad?" I said.

"Miss Baghdad is safe in an undisclosed corral."

I liked hearing official words like *undisclosed,* which only meant Manke had the mare stashed in one of his own secret canyon pens.

Then he said, "How about it, Tony? You set your hands on Shady Jane?"

"I don't know any Shady Jane. And I found them sorrels wandering in Ash Creek."

"Just by chance, they happened to be the same sorrels your pal Albert Wade just happened to have an interest in buying."

"Life is funny that way," Tony shrugged. "I haven't talked with Albert in a coon's age."

Ted stood up and cracked Tony across the face with a backhand slap. Pretty hard too. The chair rocked sideways, and for a second I thought he might topple over. I couldn't blame Ted at all for his temper getting the better of him.

Ted said, "We don't cotton to no wise

116

remarks. And you need to stop all this innocent talk when we know that's not the way things happened. It'll go better for you if you tell the truth."

He sat down and put the back of his slapping hand to his mouth.

I wanted to pound the stuffing out of Tony myself — but not enough to injure myself.

Ted's signature on the Association bylaws was number thirteen, under Ben Frymire but just before mine, which I guess could be an ill omen if I were superstitious about numbers, but I was determined not to think in such old-fashioned terms. There had been enough spooky goings-on and tall fish stories during my growing up years to last into the next century.

If it rained when the sun was shining it meant three more days of moisture. If it snowed on Easter, it meant it would rain for the next seven Sundays.

I'd seen that one happen though, so maybe it didn't count.

The old ladies spread the tales thicker than pig lard, but some stuff came from the Indians.

Daxte-Wau, the Sioux deer lady, would sneak into people's cabins at night to seduce the menfolk. The enormous, curving tusks of the hairy elephant monster, Pasnuta,

117

buried in the white Niobrara chalk, would come to life every alternate Sunday.

The Niobrara River land was cursed by an old Ponca medicine man because of that sorry tribe's exile in '77, and I didn't blame anybody for believing it because those men and women were terrible abused — but there wasn't anything dark and magical floating about it.

If anything, the curse of the Niobrara was like a seed that grew in any one person's heart or mind.

It was up to each of us to weed our individual gardens.

I stopped my woolgathering and looked back at Tony's face, seeing it bloom red where Ted hit him. He poked at the inside of his cheek with his tongue. Our eyes locked, and I thought he was about to spit blood on Manke's rug, but I gave him a slight shake of the head. It wasn't like I wanted him gunned down on the spot.

Next to me, Ted Roberts shook out his hand, then put a spoonful of sugar in his cup. I thought maybe he was hooked on the junk. Turned out later I was right; he ate sugar in everything, the way a normal fellow might use salt. That wasn't Ted's only vice.

"Now that we've got this little no-account,

what do we do with him?" Ted said.

As always, Cap had the answer.

His voice was low and calm, and it reminded me how Trudy sometimes talked to me about money or provisions when times were tough. Cap Burnham kept emotion out of his words, and laid out the facts to Tony Pike as we knew them to be. Nothing more to hang a grudge on, everything clean as a whistle. Hell, he was being overly kind.

"Son, we found you tending six stolen horses which your friend, a known thief, has already expressed an interest in. That doesn't look good for you. You can certainly understand our curiosity about such a thing?"

Tony held his tongue, and Cap continued with the God's honest truth.

"Nobody here wants to see you get hurt any more than you've already earned through your back talk. Seems to me, the best thing to do is come clean. Tell us about your friends. Tell us where we can find Albert Wade and the others. Tell us where we can find Shady Jane."

Tony grinned with a kind of sarcastic expression. "If I do that, I suppose you'll let me go?"

"We might just do that," Manke said. "How about let's find out."

"How about let's not?"

Ted jumped up, ready to slug him again, but Cap got between them with his words. "Sit down, Ted. It's all right."

Ted was reluctant, but a look from Manke and me convinced him. "We've got plenty of time to sweat this fellow," Manke said. "My wife is away for a few days, visiting her sister in Knox County. Long as we don't get blood on her rug, we'll be fine."

Tony turned sorta pale at the mention of blood. Ted laid his Navy Colt on the table, the business end pointed right at Tony's left tit.

That's all it took. The little thief cracked like a dropped egg.

"There's a place over in Stuart," he said. "They serve fried taters with onions. You can smell the onions a mile away. You go behind the lunch house, there's a summer kitchen where they keep the corn squeezings. Any night after sunset you might find Billy Morris there. He's the one who helped Albert with Manke's sorrels, not me."

"There now. See how easy that was?" Cap said.

I looked around the table at Manke, Cap, and Ted.

It felt good to be working with such a

good bunch of men.

We made Tony repeat everything again, and Manke wrote it all down. The onion place was an old way station for the stage run by a floozy gal named Liz. Tony figured she sold more than chow, but it didn't matter to us, who were married men, except for Ted who got sort of excited. We were getting awful used to the sordid side of life, so nothing surprised us.

After Cap figured Tony had told us everything he was going to, Manke dragged him outside and tossed him down into a root cellar in the dark. "We'll bring you a bite of breakfast presently," Cap said. Then he rubbed the back of his head. "Tony said he doesn't know where Shady Jane is, and I believe him."

Ted and I agreed with the sentiment.

When Manke got back to the table, Burnham said, "I do believe our next order of business is securing John and Albert Wade."

I said, "I can't believe they're working together."

"I understand you've got personal reason to find the old man," Manke said. He brushed at his own cheekbone, meaning to reference the dark bruises I had carried from my encounter at the cow pond.

I nodded with enthusiasm. "The man

threatened my wife and damn near killed me."

"And he also stole your milk cow, isn't that right?"

"That's right."

"I bring it up," Cap said, "because you need to know we aren't your personal vendetta squad. If you have a beef with a man, you settle it between yourselves. Of course, I know you tried to do just that."

Ted spoke up for me. "And in so doing, he learned John Wade is a crazed maniac as well as a cattle rustler."

"We can't have crazed maniacs and thieves running wild," Manke said. "Don't you worry, Gus. We'll get him."

Before we left, Burnham started tossing out ideas, suggesting we might at some point work in different groups, "depending on how things go." He singled out Manke. "Virgil will stay with me, at least until we locate Shady Jane." Then he said, "C.C. Dodge leads a group from over by Paddock."

"Makes sense. Maybe have a Keya Paha group, too," I said, just to feel included, and Burnham nodded at me. Made me warm inside.

"I'd like to see you two boys stay with Virgil and me," he said.

"I'd be pleased to do it," Ted said.

"Me too," I said.

Manke agreed. "We're a fine team."

With Tony in the cellar and the horses put away, there wasn't much more to be said.

Manke let me take the remains of the brown bottle, and I shook hands with Ted.

Singing "Red Budding Bluebells," I drank all the way to the Running Water where I fell off my horse under the morning stars.

I laid there for a while in a swoon, listening to the cold river flow, hearing a coyote throw his voice across the water so he sounded like an entire pack.

It went like that for a while. Water. Coyotes. They mixed together in layers, one on top of the other, the sounds of nature passing time.

And pretty soon, I started to shiver in the freezing cold, and all I heard was a continuous roar like the rushing of the wind high on a hill somewhere, maybe boot hill, where it was always dark nighttime and clammy like a crypt.

I don't remember anybody ever mentioning Tony Pike again.

CHAPTER NINE

From information gleaned from A.J. Burnham of Carns, captain of one of the companies of vigilants, who is here now . . . *The Ledger* is thoroughly convinced that the entire gang has been cleaned out, routed, broken up, and scattered. Quite a number of arrests have been made of horse thieves, suspicious characters, and parties whom the vigilants have obtained information against as guilty of harboring and aiding the rustlers.

There are rumors here that several citizens within the jurisdiction of the vigilants west of Burnham's company have suddenly disappeared and their whereabouts cannot be discovered. Up to the present time Captain Burnham's party have had no occasion to use any harsh measures, and they hope not to be forced to resort to any. The prisoners in their charges are treated well, and are allowed all the liberties their cases will warrant.

The Stuart Ledger, by way of the *Holt County Banner,* November 1883

Those first weeks of November, Billy Morris was arrested by Henry Richardson over at Floozy Liz's place where they cooked onions, then Billy gave up Culbertson, who ended up getting caught at Middleton's Canyon on Holt Creek. Cap Burnham snatched up McFarlin, the Carns postmaster, for being mixed up in all of this devilry, and I was tickled to see bad men shipped out of the country. Tickled to be part of it.

But we still hadn't found John Wade.

Or Shady Jane.

One fine day I picked up Baron Hale at Fairfield Creek for aiding and abetting the crooks — a fancy way of saying he fixed supper for them one night, but our tolerance for these rats was rubbing awful thin. That went double for any dumb SOB lending them a hand and making it easier for them to do their dirty work.

Ted said it best later that night when we shared a drink at the bar at Tarbell's store in Carns.

As usual, Tarbell was off cleaning a fish or tanning a hide or something, and Cap had the place open for us with Ted behind the bar.

I had kicked off my boots because they were covered with mud, and my hat sat crown-down on the long walnut bar top. With my sock foot touching the floor and my other foot propped on a second stool in front of me, I sat on a wood stool polishing my six-shooter. All my cartridges were accounted for, and as I held the gun up to the lantern light, the barrel gleamed silver orange and amber gold.

Ted dunked half his face into a tankard of beer before coming up for air, all foamy-mouthed. "You know how evil gets its hooks into you, August John? It's when good folks turn a blind eye to wrongdoing. Without the county's good Christians nurturing the garden of weeds — there wouldn't be any weeds raised up. You take this Hale character, for example."

"Took him is what I did," I said. "Without so much as firing a shot."

I dropped my gun into my leather belt rig and drank from my beer and breathed in the thick smell of hickory smoke chuffing from the split seam on the stovepipe in the corner. Cap had coffee brewing and had promised us a slab of bacon, but I hadn't seen it yet.

"You're a better man than me," Ted said.

In the warm silence of his grin, I didn't argue.

"Right after you reported in, Manke sent me over to burn down Hale's barn." He said it like somebody might tell you he picked up his mail or watered his dog. No big thing. "I watched it a while. It was glorious." Ted was always Manke's right hand.

We sat and drank, and I wondered how Trudy was, way up north at Pleasant Valley. It had been a few days since I was last home, and I was lonely for her kisses. Her warm touch.

Ted sipped and began to sermonize.

"Here's the thing to understand. We're in a contest of wills for the soul of our new county. Manke said the same. Frymire knows it. Cap sees it sometimes, but not always."

"I guess so."

"There's five thousand immigrants from all over just itching to come here and plant their feet in our good Brown County soil. Some of them are good people. Sturdy people with families who want to build something. And some of them may not be such good people. But you know what, Gus? All of them are 'fraid to come here. If we're not careful, word will get out to the bad men that this is the place to set up shop."

"You think so?"

Ted's expression assured me he did. "I don't think — I know. The *Stuart Ledger* says good folks won't bring good livestock into Brown, Holt, or Knox Counties. Says the settlers are going north to Dakota or south to the Platte. Until we get things cleaned up, the Niobrara is cursed."

"I don't read the papers."

"You should. You owe it to yourself to know what folks are saying."

"I don't care what folks are saying."

"They'll carve that shit on your tombstone."

"Uh-huh."

I wasn't really listening.

My longing overpowered the woodsmoke. My mind wandered to the lavender, clean smell of Trudy's hair. In memory, her voice drowned out Ted's well-worn diatribes. How long had it been since I'd been home?

Ted said, "Once Cap sees that it's you and me on one side, the settlers and sodbusters on the other, we can make some progress. Once we go against the settlers, we'll make some real progress."

I caught a tone of scorn in the words, and it woke me up.

"What do you mean, *against* the settlers?"

"Those poor idiots don't know who to trust. In some ways, they're as dangerous as the owlhoots we're trying to round up."

I said, "The way I see it, we're working *for* the settlers and sodbusters, not *against* them."

Ted looked down his nose at me through his impossibly thick specs — like I was thick in the head.

"It's a cute way to think, and I reckon I had similar notions early on. But you wait and see, August John. You'll see I'm right."

It set my jaw on edge, him being so smug, and I thought about just pulling out my bedroll in the corner and calling it a night. We'd all been so busy tearing thunder across the country, never staying two days in the same place, I could sleep in the funnel of a tornado and be thankful for the rocking motion of the wind.

All told, I think there were twenty or thirty of us working with Cap at that time.

But Ted Roberts was starting to sour on me. Like Tarbell's beer.

My growling stomach kept me from bedding down. Where the hell was Cap with our late-night supper?

Ted said, "You get a few more weeks of the hunt for these miscreants under your belt, you'll see what I mean about people sheltering them."

"I already know what you mean." I wanted him to drop it. "I thought Cap was bringing in supper?"

"Aw, you know Cap. He probably got to jawing with Hale about cattle prices or seed corn." Ted leaned in close and lowered his voice. "You ask me, there's more efficient ways to sweat a man."

I dropped down to the wood floor in my stocking feet. "I'm going to go find out what's keeping them."

Anything to get away from Ted's endless preaching.

Tarbell's store was a bigger concern than our little place at Pleasant Valley, but even so, it only had three rooms: one big mercantile area with the saloon counter, an apartment with a bed and second stove where Tarbell lived, and a narrow, cramped office with a heavy wooden door.

I found Cap in the third room with Baron Hale, rapping on the table situated between them, rocking the lone candle that supplied a dim light, emphasizing a point.

The two of them were talking baseball.

"You know Myron Berry can outpitch your pal Culbertson any day of the week."

Hale wasn't convinced. "Says you."

"Says you, nothing. You'll see next summer."

There was nothing sinister about the young German. Nothing to say he'd thrown his lot in with a ring of bad men. In fact, I'd barely had reason to coax him from his sod home at gunpoint and bring him to Carns. All I'd had was the Word.

But in those days, in that place, the Word was all powerful, passed from one whispering jenny to another. One mouth to one ear, over and over again. Baron Hale had made supper for Culbertson. Gave a slice of ham to Eph Weatherwax. Cooked taters for John Wade.

The Word was big enough to hang a man.

Cap leaned back in his chair when I walked in. "Mr. Hale says he's never once met John Wade. But I'm pretty sure he fits the description of a known associate who's been covering tracks for him."

I sized the fellow up, tried to imagine him with a dark hat and maybe a three-day ring of whiskers over his baby smooth cheeks. His blond hair was combed, his teeth, white as a virgin's soul. I imagined him more unkempt . . . but wasn't sure.

"Maybe we made a mistake," I said.

And when I said it, the look in Hale's eyes proved we hadn't. Cap saw it, too — the defiance.

"Nope. This is the man."

I unbuttoned my holster and withdrew my gun. I handed it over to Cap. "Wanna hold this for me?"

"I can do that." The tone of his voice posing a question I immediately answered.

I walked around the table and cracked my knuckles beside Hale's ear. Then I slapped him across the mouth. Open handed, not hard.

Hale nudged his lip with his tongue and tasted blood. He glared at me, so I hit him again.

Cap said, "That's enough, Gus."

"Not by far," I said. "This bastard knows where John Wade is, and you've been sitting in here chattering with him like it's the Lutheran Ladies' Aid."

"Don't you take a tone with me, boy."

"It wasn't you who John Wade left to die. It wasn't your wife he came for."

Now the hair on Cap's neck was raised too, and his neck flushed red in the flickering light. My hand whipped out to snatch my gun, but Cap was faster, pulling it away. "Oh, no," he said. "If you're louse enough to savage a man when he's sitting down, I'm not giving back your gun."

I turned on my heel to face Hale. "What

do you think, Mr. Hale? Do you think I'm a louse?"

What had been a relatively dry scalp when I strolled into the room, now beaded up damp, and sweat trickled down the side of Hale's face.

"Stand up," I said, but he stayed in his seat.

"*Geh zum Teufel,* Gus." Go to the Devil.

"I'm going to ask you once about John Wade," I said, "and if you tell me a lie, I'm going to drive my fist into the side of your face and break your jaw."

Staring straight ahead, Hale kept his fingers laced in his lap. He set his teeth into a hard grimace.

I glanced at Cap, then back to Hale. I said, "Do you know John Wade?"

The German cleared his throat. "Yes," he said. "I know John Wade."

"And do you know where he is right now?"

"If I did, I would not tell you —"

"Do you know where he is!"

Then the dirty kraut blinked and turned his face to me. He smiled.

"*Jawohl,*" he said. Yes.

I balled up my fist, clenching my fingers until the knuckles were white.

"Tell me."

Slow at first, he wagged his head. Then

faster. *"Nein."*

My fingernails dug through the skin of my palms until they were stained with blood.

"I told you what I would do to you."

Again with the defiant grin.

"Leck mich am arsch."

When we walked out of the room together, Cap put his arm around my sagging shoulders.

"Go clean yourself up," he said.

I was covered in sweat and stood short and hunched over.

I massaged my battered, bloody knuckles, wanting to throw up.

Ted met us at the bar. "What happened in there?"

Cap said, "Get Gus a shot of something good and strong."

"But what happened?"

"We've got him," was all I said as I stumbled toward the door and the frigid cold air outside, guts heaving.

Cap said, "We've got John Wade."

And sometime during the next few days, Baron Hale disappeared forever.

CHAPTER TEN

"Fourteen, fifteen miles northeast of Carns," Baron Hale told me, through shattered, bloodstained teeth. "John Wade's hardwood claim is nothing but a sorry heap of mud and trees."

He said Wade would be there, likely boozing it up or diddling some gal beside his broke-down woodstove. Wade was still married to Deborah, but the girls he kept on the side were common knowledge, and it made me feel bad for Albert's mother, everybody talking like they did.

Hale told us some dun buckskins would be a hundred yards behind the moldy sod hut in a half-ass corral with some cows surrounded by cedars. At the end of the conversation, Hale said Albert and Eph Weatherwax might be on hand, too — taking target practice or playing pitch depending on how cold it was outside. Albert lived his life outside, so I was ready to be on guard. Who knows where he would jump up with his little British Bull Dog pistol or his Model 1877 Colt .38?

He could be just about any place.

Hale admitted his own part in propping up neighbors who weren't behaving in what I would call a neighborly fashion. The ring of thieves had help along the way. Otherwise, they couldn't have come so far on their own, he said.

He called Albert a *dummkopf,* but of course he was wrong about that because Albert was cagey as a fox. Maybe his teeth hurt so bad he wasn't thinking real straight. Weatherwax was almost certainly an idiot, but wasn't nobody with a better streak of luck than Eph, so things kinda evened out that way for him.

Sometimes it seemed like the good Lord Himself watched over Pony Boys, tipping fortune's trough in their direction, a sentiment Albert always shared. At least that's what Al told me later.

Naturally, it snowed overnight, making things harder for us.

Pony Boy luck that I never shared in.

The next morning Cap drove a four-in-hand from Carns with a buckboard load of provisions, and Ben Frymire rode on the spring seat next to him. We took black powder and ammunition, rope, and a rusty scattering of iron tools. Cap carried our bedrolls and a war bag full of chow — what was left from the slab of bacon and a couple dozen day-old doughnuts fried in lard. Ted Roberts and me carried our own canteens on our horses.

I rode along behind the wagon at a good clip, keeping Ed between the wheel ruts, and Ted Roberts trailed along on my right. The sky was a mix of ragged gray wool and hints of blue, and fat snowflakes swirled around every so often. Once I saw the sun and thought we were saved, but it ducked back under the covers quick enough. Like the old song about rain, the old man was snoring. Long time ago, Sonny had told me the old man in the song was the sun.

Now and then, I'd let my hand brush against the coil of rope I carried and I had my new Army Frontier snug on my hip.

Pretty much all of us had Peacemakers when we rolled into the sod claim mid-afternoon, and Ted Roberts had Cap's .50 Sharps long-barreled rifle.

A patchy shelterbelt of stubby cedars and listing pines lined the north and west of the property. The trees in the row were full of gaps and broken limbs, the wet snow weighing heavy on the branches. Tucked up close to the trees, the soggy remnant of a sod blockhouse — the east end collapsed in on itself, the opposite side tilting backwards — showed a dim light in a cracked glass window, and a thin curlicue of smoke looped out of a lone horizontal tin pipe jutting out from the snow cover. While we watched, two men came out the front door and disappeared inside the privy together. There were no additional buildings, no other fences. How any man could consider such a place home was beyond my ken.

"If there's a horse pen down there, I can't see it," I said.

Ted Roberts said it was familiar to him, telling me his uncle, Henry Richardson, had tried to buy the place once. "You're not supposed to see the horse corral. This place was designed by thieves to keep their remuda secret and safe." Ted was more and more full of himself.

When we pulled in next to Cap's wagon on a little knoll overlooking the yard, I said, "If you know your way around so well, how about you take the lead? Maybe you can handle it all by yourself." I didn't mean to sound snotty, but my nerves were on edge. It was all I could do not to rush down onto the house, hell for leather, raining lead and fire through windows and doors.

"You've got to calm yourself, Gus," Cap said. Even from the wagon seat, he could see I was excited.

"I'm just chilly," I said, smacking my gloved hands against the sleeves of my canvas brown coat. My breath came in white clouds as I said it. "Need to get some blood flowing."

"Oh, it'll flow," Ted said.

Cap barked at him. "If that's your plan, boy, you just stay up here and provide cover."

He wasn't putting up with such nonsense. Looking at each of us in turn, he said, "Gus, Ted, Ben — you boys signed an agreement."

He meant the vigs' bylaws and our obligations to do things right and proper.

Ted let his mouth run over and got slammed down for it. No way I was going to miss out on the action.

Not this time.

Not when I'd been waiting so long to get ahold of John Wade's scruffy hide.

And, yeah. Blood might flow.

But I wasn't stupid enough to say it where Cap would hear.

I held my tongue between my teeth.

Ted just sat and glared at the wagon while me and Frymire and Cap went over our approach.

"You leave your buckskin here, Gus. Walk down around the perimeter. Keep the shelterbelt between you and the house where you can. We know there's at least two men down there, sure."

Bald headed, with a Stetson two sizes too big, Frymire rarely spoke unless you lit a match under him. Given the circumstances, and since it was his horses we had sussed out, I liked to think his pants were on fire. But not so much.

He said, "I haven't seen anybody since those gents went to the outhouse." Which was his entire contribution so far. Like Cap had once said, Frymire was a true believer. I don't rightly understand what goes on in a church man's mind, but Frymire was more reserved than most.

Cap said, "Do you think either one of those fellows we saw was Wade?"

"I can't be sure," I said. "But I'm willing to go down and find out."

"You watch yourself. When you get all the way around to the back side of the privy, give us a wave. We'll leave the wagon here and slip down to the trees. I'd like to get the stolen livestock loose and drove away to pasture before we brace the gents inside."

"If there is any stolen livestock."

"There will be," Ted said. "Maybe Kid

Wade will be there too."

I snuck down through the snow, a black mark against the November white background of the day, sloshing through the crackling yellow and brown grass that poked up through the skiffs of slush.

The sky above was a roiling sea of blue and white and scudding gray clouds. Halfway to the cedars, it occurred to me what an easy target I was for anyone who might be looking this way from the sod house window. I was a black bug inching across a bleached paper hill. But I made it to the first windbreak okay, and after that, slipping from tree to tree through the muffled grove kept me hid well enough.

Everything was quiet, and the breeze barely touched me. The snow was dry here, more powdery where the fickle sun hadn't sent any heat at all. My heart was pounding away like a marching band's kid drummer who never before picked up a stick.

Between the branches, I got a closer look at the house, a site of such sickness and blight, I wanted nothing more than to pull my Frontier model and deliver all six slugs of mercy to the place — put it out of its misery. But then my attention was caught by a soft murmur and shuffling of hooves. The blowing of bovine air. Through the trees behind the house, I could make out a pen with around half a dozen cows. My Betty was one of them.

Closing in, I heard a whinny, thought I'd found Shady Jane herself, but it was a free-standing black mare between me and the house. She was a gorgeous horse with an ivory blaze down her face and a voluptuous shiny tail and mane. I recognized her as belonging to Tarbell, the storekeeper.

The mare perked up her ears and stamped when I snuck past, but nobody was paying attention. Once I got up to the privy, I poked my head around and waved to Cap.

That's when I heard the giggling coming from inside the shack.

I palmed my Colt and crept around to the side, sure now there were at least two fellows inside. I didn't recognize their voices as anybody I knew, but either way nobody likes to be surprised in the middle of privy business, and who knows if they were armed?

At the same time, I couldn't wait forever.

When I peeked back around the corner, sure enough, there was Cap trundling down the hill in a kind of sideways skid, haranguing the team of four horses. They came near to falling one on top of another ass over teakettle, but Cap got them straight and

Frymire flanked him on my buckskin, Ed. We'd be in a world of hurt if we lost the horses, plunked down out here in the armpit of nowhere. If John Wade was inside the house and looked out his front window, he'd start shooting.

Which is precisely when I heard the first big boom.

I thought sure I'd called it right, that it was Wade plinking away from his front door, but a heavy thud came from the side of the sod house closest to me and chaff exploded up in ten directions, damping down the tomfoolery going on inside the outhouse.

Damned if Ted Roberts didn't trigger a second blast of Cap's big gun, causing Wade's black pony to dance and snort. I was lucky it took him a minute to reload.

Now I was the one caught short.

Either I'd have to shoot those gents in the privy, or they'd bust out and shoot me. One of 'em said, "C'mon, Willy!" and from the accent, I knew it was Swede Carlson. The other one must've been Willy Ransom.

I caught sight of a hunk of limestone rock the size of a Thanksgiving pumpkin, half-covered in snow but loose enough to kick over without even thinking. I dropped my iron and used both arms to hoist the rock up and sway it over to where it landed with a whump against the outhouse door just as the occupants pushed from inside.

Helpless to move the heavy weight, they complained. "Who's out there?"

Then: "You rotten dog!"

"Your life is over, coward."

And on and on.

I picked up my gun and fired at the doorjamb. The shack rocked backwards as my prisoners fell over against the back wall. "You boys just stay put until the killing's done," I warned. "You might survive long enough to be embarrassed."

To their credit, no further comments were offered in the silence that followed, and I hustled up to the rear window of the house.

Cupping my face against the outside glare, I pushed my nose to the glass and saw John Wade stumbling out of bed, twisted up in a threadbare, torn sheet and ratty quilt, tugging a pair of black trousers from a chair while his yellow dog paced across the mattress.

Another rifle shot broke through the front window, and this time I cursed Ted Roberts out loud. If he wasn't careful, he'd hit one of his friends.

At the time I was too busy to consider he might not think of all of us as his friends.

I crashed the barrel of my pistol through

the fragile little window and Wade spun around, saw the gun, and lunged for the front door, still naked from the waist up. It was pointless to waste a bullet, so I started around the house in the direction he ran, but came right up against Ben Frymire on Ed.

"He's on the run," I said.

Frymire jumped off the buckskin, his own six-shooter in hand. At the same time, Wade had changed direction, rounded the far side of the soddy, slipped in the snow, but kept his balance long enough to launch himself onto the back of Tarbell's black horse.

I had just enough time to catch the look of raw terror on his face before he whirled his mount around and took off through the trees.

"I'll get him," I said, leaping onto Ed's back. "Tell Cap. There's two more in the outhouse."

Cedar boughs scratched my face, and I lost my hat ducking through the pines, but if John Wade thought anything was going to stop me, he was wrong. I still had Baron Hale's blood under my fingernails, still heard his groans in the back of my head. I paid for access to this sonuvabitch; I wasn't gonna quit now.

I was so hungry for vengeance in those

first few seconds of the chase, I might've blown out John Wade's heart with a shot to the back had the trees not been in the way.

I'm not proud to say it — who would be?

But I cooled off when we hit the open range, and thought about those Association bylaws. What can I say — my thinking it through saved his life.

For a little while, anyway.

CHAPTER ELEVEN

Back in Doc Middleton's day there were pony boys and there were *Pony Boys* and the distinction between the two was subtle; but, for a brief window of time, this distinction was not lost on the folks on the Niobrara.

Any man jack or squirrel could rope off a string of half-starved wild horses and flip 'em to the pioneers for a dollar. Sometimes a fellow would need some fast coin and taking a quick colt away from an Indian or "accidently" coming home with a friend's horse from the saloon was an easy way to do it.

Amateurs came and went and always will. Folks who lost a horse took to saying "one of them pony boys must've got it."

Professionals — the Pony Boys — stayed the course and didn't get caught.

And while there wasn't any law in the unorganized west, there was plenty of public sentiment. Professionals stayed in their neighbors' good graces.

Doc always said: A wise dog don't shit in its neighbor's backyard. Them who did got what they had coming, and it was never pleasant.

If there was a fence to be mended or a barn to be raised, we usually showed up. If a man was sick and needed a tonic, one of us had a fast horse to fetch the medicine. Doc Middleton rode ten hours once to help deliver a baby, and he worked three days to save a man who had fallen into a well.

Us who circled around Doc Middleton's sun got to calling ourselves the Pony Boys — with uppercase letters like it was a name we could be proud of, at least me and Albert and some others did. We tried to make a clear distinction between the sticky fingered snot-nosed kids who pilfered sick livestock and broke-down nags. Them we called scalpers, and it had nothing to do with Indians. It was butchering a man's wallet.

We were damned good at the skills we had.

The skill alone separated the lowercase pony boys from the uppercase crew.

As John Wade rode the bare back of his black mare, bouncing over the range with a loud frenzy of slapping and hollering and carrying on with a froth at the mouth, I was cool and biding my time, judging my distance, feeling each fiber in the coil of rope between my fingers.

When Manke said I should challenge Ben Frymire in the next roping contest, I had acted all humble and toe-in-the-dust, but Virgil was right.

Frymire was the second best man I knew with a rope.

Because I was the first.

The black mare shot past a wild patch of ragweed and tore through an open meadow kicking up frosty clots of black mud and yellow straw. If Wade meant to escape by a flat-out marathon, me and Ed were more than up for the task. Straight ahead in the far-off distance was the Running Water, and after that, the long open stretch to the Sandhills. There wasn't any place to hide.

We had plenty of time to match him step for step. All I needed was for Wade to sit up a bit, put himself straight. My rage tempered by the steady, cool run, I honestly didn't want to make a hangman's throw and snap his neck.

The rope circled around my grip, a nice rhythm, mixing in with the gallop of my horse, a spiritual tempo. Riding with a lasso, breathing high plains air and counting the beats, well — that was church to me. It was all the religion I needed. Trudy endeavored to teach me the Bible, but I'd already been saved by the saddle. What was it Jesus said, "I'll make you fishers of men?"

After all, wasn't that what I was doing? Wasn't I fishing?

To my way of thinking, if Jesus had lived in Nebraska, he'd make people swing a rope.

I let the loop fly. God was on my side. Vengeance was ours.

The spinning wide loop twirled through the air, drawn down by gravity and earth and holy righteousness, then draped down over Wade's shoulders and I pulled tight.

Snap.

Tarbell's mare didn't like having her rider jerk backwards, his feet flying up to brush her ears as Wade made a desperate grab at her withers. Skidding in the slush and snow of the wide open field, she threw her head forward and down, then reared up on her hind legs, dumping Wade down flat before spinning in a circle.

I reined in and let Ed drag our lurching, twisted bounty across the frozen scrub several yards away from Tarbell's cranky mare.

Wade bared his teeth and screamed, more in humiliation than pain. At one point he got both hands up above his head and grasped the rope, using it to lever himself partway upright.

I had the hemp wrapped around Ed's saddle horn and returned the pull, dumping Wade face-first into a saw-blade patch of grass.

"Keep it up, Wade. We'll have a fun afternoon, you and me."

"I shoulda killed you —"

"When you had the chance? Yeah. You should've, you dumb sumbuck."

"I'll still make you sorry. You and that whore you live —"

This time I slapped Ed's rump and let him trot a good distance. "Hard to talk with a jaw full of frozen loam and broken teeth."

I guess I remembered Wade slamming my face down again and again into the cow pond.

He'd really enjoyed that. The way some men liked watching a horse race or playing cards.

Some fellows like to drink and some play the piano.

John Wade snookered horses and beat people up, but in my heart I guess I knew he was more than just a rotter. Trudy said he wasn't all bad, and it's what saved him from me — her gentle, consistent voice piping up between my fits of retribution.

That, and the fact Cap and his bylaws would frown on me bringing Wade in dead as a hammer. At the cedar belt, I drew Ed to a standstill and waited while Wade hauled his bruised, aching carcass up to his full height.

He stood swaying like a willow sapling, and I said a quick prayer against a strong wind.

"John Wade, I'm detaining you in the name of the Niobrara Mutual Protection Association for the crime of horse thievin' and stealing my milk cow."

His head bobbed around, nodding or maybe just shaking off the rattles inside his skull. "You . . . got it all figured out, don't you? You think playing two ends . . . against the middle makes you . . . a big man. You damned hypocrites."

"Don't know what makes you say that," I said.

Wade shook his head. "You all are bigger horse thieves than I'll ever be."

"You want to lead us to Shady Jane?"

"You ask your friends about that."

"Mister, your head ain't on straight." I gave him a gentle tug, and we walked a few yards back toward the house.

"You boys got a good thing going, it don't matter to me." He yanked the rope two times, hard in succession, and I stopped again to look back and listen.

"You got something to say, you say it."

Bent over with his hands on both knees, I thought he would be sick. My lasso was more than a little snug around his middle, and bloody. Maybe digging into his guts too tight. When he rose up, he seemed more clearheaded.

"I think I'll let you all work it out between yourselves."

"I don't know what you think you know —"

"I just want out of the whole thing. You take those duns in the pen. Take your milk cow back to your whore."

"I thought I was done busting your filthy mouth. Guess maybe it needs some more work." I gigged Ed forward just quick enough to pull Wade over onto his face.

He hit the ground with a thud, and when he turned over, his expression went from conniving deal-maker to a desperate man putting his life in my hands.

"Cut me loose," he hissed.

"I can't do that," I said.

"Goddamn, you! Are you boys gonna hang me right here then? Is that the plan?"

"Ain't nobody gonna get hanged today, Mr. Wade. We're taking you and your pals in to Stuart where you'll stay with the Justice of the Peace there. Mr. Gates has already agreed to watch over you until a hearing can be arranged on Monday."

Wade's eyes were defiant and he chewed at his broken lips. "I'll tell the judge every damn thing I know about you people. About Shady Jane and your entire stinking crew. You're more horse thieves than I've ever been."

"What about Swede Carlson and Willy Ransom? That's who we're gonna find back at your place, ain't we? You gonna vouch for them, say they weren't horse thieves?"

"Willy's my cousin."

I scratched the back of my head, tilting my hat forward. "I'll say this for you, Wade. You got more cousins than old Abraham."

"They're just kids."

"You need to get straight with your story."

"Afraid I'll give you up, aren't you, Gus?"

"What can you give up? You're spinning wool out of thin air."

As we sat there in the cold November day, him bare-chested and beat to hell, me warm in my coat on top of Ed, all I could do was wonder what kind of fear would drive a man to such bald-faced lies when everybody knew it was the truth that set men free.

CHAPTER TWELVE

"I brought Betty back to you, just like I promised."

Trudy nuzzled my neck in response, and I moved my shoulder on the soft straw mattress to better accommodate her in the crook of my arm. "Don't leave home again," she said.

"I'm not planning to."

Morning sunlight streamed through the back window of our house at Pleasant Valley, casting four square panes of brilliance across the chair at the foot of our bed, across my sweat-stained blue cotton shirt, jeans, and underthings. It made my head hurt.

"I drank too much last night," I said.

"Bringing in John Wade, you had good reason to celebrate." Trudy brushed the hair away from my cool, dry forehead. She wanted to say more. She held back.

"What?"

"Nothing. Just . . . nothing."

"After we turned Wade over to the Justice in Stuart, I volunteered to stick around and add my testimony at the legal hearing. Cap said it wasn't necessary, but I stayed the extra day, just to make sure all was secure."

"The regulators can get along without you now for a while."

"Cap planned to be there to bring charges. Don't forget, he's a full-fledged attorney. Really it's just a formality because they'll be shipping Wade off to West Point for his eventual trial with some of the other crooks from Brown County — us not being all set up yet for official jurisprudence."

She lifted her upper body up on her right elbow and the quilt and sheet fell away enough to reveal a husband's private scenery. She put a gentle index finger on my lips. "Let's hear no more about it." Much as I enjoyed the view, I couldn't get past the fog in my brain.

"You should've heard the things Wade said to me."

She kept her finger pressed down. "Shush."

I kissed her hand. "Don't you want to hear?"

"All I need to know is you're safe." Her hair spilled down on me from behind her ear, and her lips caught mine in a firm embrace. "John will be sent to jail, and we can get on with our life. It's why you went off with Burnham. I understand that, but now you're done."

I propped myself up on both elbows to meet her, feeling more at home now than ever before, knowing she was right.

Knowing she didn't need to be concerned. Not anymore.

I didn't want to go out again for a long time.

At least a couple weeks.

My arms started to shake from the effort of sitting up. "I sure could use a drink."

"Not now."

I drifted back down to the mattress under the gentle caress of her experienced hands. "You're full of knots. Roll over, I'll rub your back."

I did as she asked. "I'm . . . glad to be home." I felt the emotion rise up in my chest like a wave of ocean water and my eyes and nose were tight with the tide. "I'm so glad to be home."

A tear dropped to my pillow and I buried my face, hoping Trudy didn't see. I wasn't the kind to cry, and especially not in front of my wife. What would she think of it? What a weakling!

I clamped down and said, "I'm sorry."

"It's alright," she said, and her voice sort of pulled a plug on a tub fill of tension right there. I thought I'd done a good job of losing the strain the night before when we first bedded down — at least as much as I could remember. Sleeping with Trudy's warm rump pressed up against me had brought a dreamless, deep rest.

But now I truly released it all. Everything I'd kept pent up while we were questioning Tony Pike and Baron Hale. Everything burned out on the downhill slope approaching John Wade's house and the mad dash chasing him across the muddy meadow.

I bawled like a two-year-old kid and felt ashamed.

When nothing was left but the sobbing, Trudy knelt above me and kissed the back of my neck and shoulders. She put her hands on my back and kneaded away the final lumps, calmed the burden I still carried.

"It's all over," she said. "Now you can concentrate on the job at hand."

I sighed, luxuriating in the fluid motion of her fingers, the snug peace of my feather pillow. Even my headache started to clear. "I'll get to work on that pile of timber tomorrow," I said. "Leave it to a woman to remind a weary man about his to-do list."

"Turn over here," she said, playful, nearly flipping me onto my back with a simple poke to the ribs.

I rolled over with a laugh, "Hey, that tickles," and she sat back on her haunches in the sunlight.

The blankets slipped clean away.

"Raising a barn wasn't the work I was talking about," she said.

I thought there might be a joke someplace in there about raising something up or maybe about timber wood. But I was too distracted to think straight.

An hour later, we drank coffee in the adjacent room, me wearing nothing but my jeans, Trudy dressed in my shirt and wearing knitted yarn slippers. The cookstove blazed away in the corner, and a tall, well-stacked pile of split hickory and elm waited in the corner for their turn to roast. Trudy saw me notice the inventory.

"Sonny's a good man with an axe. He's kept me in kindling and even shot a couple rabbits."

"I knew he'd take care of you."

"We've had it rough with you gone so much. Nobody comes around anymore. Timmons hasn't made a grain delivery for weeks."

"Ted Roberts said that Timmons might've been mixed up with some cattle rustling over at Paddock."

"He's just another one of the vanished." She said it so matter-of-fact, the statement didn't register with me. Let alone the phrase. I should have asked her right then what she meant by *vanished.*

Instead, I relaxed against the back of my wooden rocking chair and sipped from my cup.

"Other than tending Betty, we might stay inside all day."

She padded over to stand beside me. Then she kissed my cheek. "I think we should stay in the back room." I stood up and held her tight in my arms.

We both knew what the other had in mind. We were playful about lovemaking, even frivolous. But underneath, as Trudy had suggested in bed, there was a job to be done.

Watching her scurry around the stove and counter, gathering up smoked bacon and fresh eggs for breakfast, I was an eager hand.

"I'm yours to command for the day," I said.

And then somebody else called out for attention.

"Halloo, the house! Anybody at home?"

160

Trudy froze in mid-motion. She pushed the slab of bacon to one side with a wry smile, setting her cup down gently.

Sonny's familiar voice came again from the other side of our front door. "You in there, August John? Trudy?"

"Should we let him in, or make him stand out there on the stoop?" I said.

"He's looking for attention."

"He's looking for breakfast is what he is."

"He and I got into a fine habit of breakfast while you were away drinking."

I didn't like the sound of that — especially the drinking part — and my face must've said so, because Trudy put her hand on her creamy smooth hip, and said, "Sorry?"

"Maybe."

"Stay home from now on."

I couldn't argue with her there. But just to be ornery, I made the door in two, quick strides. "You might want to get dressed," I said, flinging the door open wide.

"Gus!" Trudy squealed with surprise and made a lunge for the back room, awkward like a cat on a frozen lake.

It felt good to tease each other — like we did when we first married.

She clamped the back room door closed behind her, and I laughed, and turned, and said, "Holy cow, Sonny, I think you —"

161

The words caught in my throat.

I literally went blank for something to say.

Sonny had brought company with him to breakfast.

Ben Frymire straightened his back in his thick brown jacket, and Biff Barlow's cheeks were pink as the tip of his nose. Bashful, he looked in every direction except straight ahead.

If Frymire in his jacket, slim denim pants, and tall Stetson was a surprise, seeing him at my door on a Monday morning with Biff Barlow, the confidence man we'd chased out of Long Pine, was a shock.

Sonny stood there, helpless, like a ten-year-old kid with a question on his face, not sure if I'd hold him in contempt. "It's your partners in crime come to call, don't you see?" He tried to laugh it off, hoping I wouldn't be upset. "They just now rode up, Gus."

Frymire said, "Shut up, Sonny."

"Here now," I told him. "That's no way to say good morning."

Frymire pushed out his bottom lip like he was judging at hog at the county fair. Wagged his head when it didn't measure up. "Good's in how you look at things. Ain't much good for me in it."

"Reckon I'd say the same thing about your

friend here," I said.

Dressed in a blue undershirt and bib overalls, Biff didn't wear a coat, insulated as he was by nature. I remembered him on the edge of the cow pond, wild-eyed, hooting about gold and hidden treasure.

"I figured you for a better caliber of partner, Ben."

"Aw, Biff's okay," Frymire said.

Sonny said, "Can we come in?"

"Trudy's just . . . ah." I looked over my shoulder. The back room door was closed. "Trudy's just changing into her work clothes."

Sonny peered in, a pleading look on his face. "Biff's your neighbor, after all."

I didn't know where the hell Biff Barlow lived.

I said, "What brings you up this way, Ben?"

"Horse business. More or less."

Tired of waiting for an invitation, Frymire brushed past me, kicking his bootheels against the dirt floor of our kitchen space with a clump, clump, clump.

"You like living in two rooms?" he said. He stamped hard on the ground beside the table. "You ought to use that pile of wood outside to build a civilized floor."

The challenge in his eyes was both real

163

and imagined. Part of me wanted to agree and get right to work, measuring boards and sawing lumber and laying down that floor. The other part knew it was just his way.

Frymire was generally quiet and reserved. It didn't mean he didn't hold deep-seated opinions. And when they showed up, they tended to come off the cuff — rapid fire like the chatter of a woodpecker.

But what's funny is he really did think I should build a floor for Trudy.

"I've got all sorts of plans for this place," I assured him. "I should say, we both do, me and Trudy."

"Sounds good to me," Frymire said, under his breath. "Keep your ass busy at home, you won't be hightailing around the country with the Niobrara regulators."

"I guess I could say the same to you," I said.

Sonny plopped down in a chair like he owned the place. "You boys have a seat."

Frymire went around the table and pulled out a stool. He removed his Boss of the Plains, put it down on the floor beside him, then sat down with his back against the wall, in the same place Kid Wade always used to sit when he'd come to Trudy's store for coffee and biscuits.

Biff was more tentative, touching the

164

crown of a high-backed chair. "This okay?" he said.

"Take a load off," Sonny said.

Biff wasn't sure.

"It's fine," I told him. "Nobody's gonna bite you."

He sat down between Sonny and Frymire. "Obliged to you. I sure do know you have no reason to trust the likes of me."

"Forget them horse apples," Frymire said. Then he told me, with a tilt of his head, "Biff and his sisters moved into the old Darren place back yonder." He hooked a thumb toward the east. "They've reformed. No more tricking good people."

Sonny nudged Biff. "Get them sisters of yours to make me a chocolate cake. Make one for Ben too. He's been alone too long."

Frymire said, "Do I have to ask you to leave?"

"I'm gonna have all three of you out of here on the toe of my boot," I said, "if you don't tell me the reason for your visit." I tried to be good-natured about it, like I was kidding, but I was annoyed as all get-out with the intrusion. Trudy and I needed time together to help close up the gulch that had grown between us.

Sonny said, "Can't a neighbor just drop in?"

"You ain't wearing any boots," Frymire said.

"I'll toss you out on your rear ends —"

Biff snatched the round hat off his head and dropped it into his lap with an apologetic glance in my direction. "Best tell him, Ben. Tell him what's happened."

Frymire took a deep breath, let it out slow. "Your wife ought to hear this too. She knew John Wade better than we did."

"What about Wade?" I said, crossing over to the stove.

Sonny said, "Is that breakfast I smell?"

I pulled three tin cups off the shelf and wiped the dust out with a cloth. "You boys want some coffee?"

"Won't say no to whatever warm stuff you're drinking today," Sonny said. "In case you didn't notice, that's a nippy wind outside."

"I noticed." I really needed to get a shirt on.

Before I had the cups full of coffee, Trudy came out of the bedroom. "Hello, boys." She crossed over to the table, greeting Frymire with a smile. "How you been, Ben?"

He brushed away Trudy's attention like she was a fly buzzing him, or a big sister. "I'm fine, I'm fine." Then he gave her a genuine look of happy affection. "It's good to see you again, Trudy. This here is Biff Barlow."

Biff stood up with an abrupt nod. "It's a pleasure, ma'am."

I said, "You remember Biff, honey. He's the scoundrel we ran out of Bassett for fleecing good Christian people."

"I've repented of all that, Gus. I truly have."

Trudy smiled. "You just sit and have some coffee, Mr. Barlow."

"You got anything stronger than coffee?" Sonny asked.

Trudy's answer seemed more directed at me than him. "As it turns out, we do not."

I carried the sloshing tin cups to the table, put them down, and sat across from Frymire. Then I bent over to pick up my boots.

Trudy brought a shirt for me out of the back room, and I put it on while Biff looked at the rifle hanging over the doorframe. Frymire gave me a satisfactory nod, then finally turned his attention to the reason for his visit.

"John Wade is dead," he said.

CHAPTER THIRTEEN

"How can Wade be dead? They were having a legal hearing today in Stuart. Burnham and some of the others were planning to be on hand."

Frymire's voice dropped down, sharing a confidence. "There's no chance of a hearing now. It never got that far. *They* took him from the Stuart Justice of the Peace on Saturday night."

"Who took him?"

"A posse of armed men with black canvas sacks over their heads. Broke down the Gateses' family door and wrestled Wade outside. These men had big Navy revolvers. There was no arguing with them."

I put down my coffee cup and wrapped my fingers around Trudy's nervous hand. She returned the squeeze.

I asked Frymire, "Did they hang him?"

"Nobody knows. Nobody's seen Wade since they drove him away in their wagon."

Trudy's words came hard as did her physical reaction — I had to wiggle my fingers, she squeezed them so tight. "Wade is one of the *vanished* now. Like so many who go missing."

I said, "Who were they? How many of them?"

"Four or five. Don't rightly know who they were." Frymire drank from his cup, then leveled his eyes across the table. "Some folks say one of them was you, Gus."

"Me? I was with Cap Burnham at the hotel on Saturday night —"

"Drinking," Frymire said. "I know. But nobody remembers exactly when you left."

"I didn't leave. I went to bed at the hotel. Around nine o'clock. Took off for home yesterday morning."

"Nobody mentioned any of this to you before you left town?"

"I was out before sunup." I didn't see any reason to keep going down the road Frymire was driving, so I backed up the conversation. "You're telling me a bunch of masked men just broke past the Justice —"

"And took Wade out, yes. They carted him off in the direction of the river."

"You don't know Wade's dead. These rascals — whoever they are — might've just taken him off to sweat him some."

169

Biff spoke up then, his voice cracking, but sure. "I was there on the street when they drug Wade to the wagon. Two of them were cursing, whipping him with their belts. Believe you me, if they delivered on half the things they promised him — Mr. Wade will never sing another song."

Which was a strange thing to say.

"Who do you think it was, Biff?"

Biff looked out the south window across the open valley, then back at his coffee cup. Again, he glanced at the rifle.

Addressing his behavior, I said, "You expectin' somebody else to come along and answer?"

Frymire said, "Being straight with you, Gus. Biff doesn't trust you. I'm not sure I do either."

Biff said, "As it happened, I'll admit I wasn't so sure it wasn't you, Gus."

My shoulders pulled tight across the back of my neck.

"And I'll be straight with both of you. I was inside the hotel, fast asleep. When have I given you reason to doubt me?"

Frymire's voice filled with caution. "Don't you crawl up on your tall horse and look at us. Ain't any one time you let us down."

"Then . . . what?"

"It's more a general sense of . . . I don't

know." He shrugged. "Drunkenness."

"Drunkenness." I nodded. "I see. I'm not to be trusted because I tip the rum bottle."

Trudy knew me, knew my moods. "Be still, Gus."

I shook my head. "You damned church men. It always comes down to your own sense of right and wrong." Always so eager to draw a line just so somebody else can be on the wrong side of it.

"Seems like us regulators all got a dose of self-righteousness running through us. We wouldn't have signed up with Burnham if we didn't."

"We enforce the law."

"What law?"

"Common decency," I said. "Right and wrong, like we'd teach any schoolboy." I poked my index finger across the table, popping his sanctimonious bubble. "Ain't nothing wrong with sippin' a bit of rum."

Frymire brushed off my words. "You and me can settle our disagreements any time, boy. I'm here telling you the way things are with John Wade and the Association."

The iron in his words came easy, from a deep well of confidence. He wasn't scared of me or worried what anybody thought. Frymire wasn't like Cap Burnham — he didn't earn respect, he demanded it.

I kept my mouth shut — but I'll give him this — he didn't hold a grudge. And he paid a man back in kind. Burnham was an attorney, good with words, good with people. Frymire was awkward and didn't say a whole lot. But when he did, it fell with the weight of a thousand archangels.

I cleared my throat.

"What about the Association?"

"Just like you, Burnham denies knowing anything about what happened. His word is official for all the vigs."

"So you immediately believe him, but not me."

"He doesn't soak up a bottle the same way you do."

Trudy stood up and made busy pulling the coffeepot off the stove and carrying it back to the table. She topped off everybody's cup, then worked to put on a second pot.

Biff said, "Don't forget about that trip you wanted to tell 'em about."

Frymire's grim smile showed gratitude. He likely hadn't talked so much in three weeks.

"Oh, yeah — I wanted to let you know they're planning a big party at Manke's place. Virgil's missuz will be putting on a spread — devil's eggs and everything."

I used my chin to motion outside toward my construction project. "I'll have to miss out. Winter's coming on strong, and I got a barn to work on." After Ben's mewing around about my rum habit, I was sick of the whole sorry lot of them. I answered. "It's just too bad if I'm not there. You can fill me in on everything later."

"Oh, I can fill you in right now. Burnham wants to lead a couple dozen men all the way up river to Niobrara City. He's talking about a run to the Black Hills in Dakota, too. Says this could be the sweep that clears these hornets out of the nest for good."

"Before Thanksgiving?"

"Just after the weekend."

"I can think of a warmer time to do it."

"Me too." Frymire finished his coffee and slid the cup back toward Trudy. Then he said, "Which is why I'm out of it. From here on in, your Niobrara Mutual Admiration Group can go it alone. And that ain't nothing against Cap Burnham or Manke . . . or you — as long as you weren't involved in taking Wade out."

"I wasn't." I nailed Frymire and Biff to their chairs with my eyes. "I won't say it again."

"Fair enough. But I'm quits with this business."

"What about Shady Jane?"

"Oh, I still want my horse. And I wouldn't mind having a chance to slug the man who took her. You find either one, you let me know. But I'm not gonna be party to outright murder. You boys want to vanish people without legal proceedings, you count me out."

Sonny put his hand on Frymire's shoulder. "It ain't like you to quit something, Ben."

The farmer pulled away. "I've done my share. Helped bring in a few men, penned them sorrels down at Manke's place. Helped bring in John Wade — only to see him dragged away in cold blood." He reached for his hat. "Nobody can say I didn't contribute."

We stood up at the same time, and Biff followed suit.

Frymire nodded at Trudy. "I'm sorry we had to interrupt your breakfast, ma'am."

Trudy's cheeks forced a weak smile.

Frymire turned to me. "Like I said, you find Jane or the man who stole her, you let me know." He walked to the door, "Word of advice — you might want to think about your friend, Kid Wade."

"He's not my friend."

"Maybe he is, maybe he isn't, but one thing's sure. If these black-masked boys

174

were willing to take out his old man, how much more eager will they be to see Albert dead?"

My shoulders tensed again and my tongue tasted like iron. I couldn't clear my throat, and I stopped breathing. Not because he was wrong, but because he was right.

I spent two weeks looking for Kid Wade and Shady Jane, traipsing through every piney gorge and glen. When I wasn't shoving Ed to punch hooves through a crusty top layer of snow, I was trotting him along spring-fed crick bottoms or up a rocky bluff.

Off I went, with a canteen of water and sorghum-bread sandwiches wrapped in brown paper. Hi-yo! There wasn't a sign of Kid Wade or his buddies — anywhere. And the homesteaders I knew were too scared to make a peep.

Sometimes I was gone overnight, and sometimes I came home for Trudy. Sonny spent most of his time passed out in the barn. None of us talked a lot, and it got so we weren't so much alive — as living not to die, each of us in our own lonesome circle waiting for something to happen.

December brought another skiff of snow, two or three inches in the lowlands, but Frymire's words stayed with me, so I stayed with the hunt.

One day a murder of crows squalled to high heaven in a grove of trees close to Plum Creek. Searching in the direction of their squawking, I saw a break in the weeds where the snow wasn't heavy and I could explore the crick bank. It was a natural trail to the water, probably well-trod by deer, nothing odd except those loud mouth crows, and them I ignored as the sun came up over the tree line.

I leaned in from the saddle and pushed aside a low-hanging branch. Then, seeing a rotund black mass swaying just above eye level, I thought someone had draped a heavy long coat over a tree branch. In the shade of a dozen hardwoods, the shape rocked back and forth without a breeze, blue-black fidgeting followed by the flutter of a wing here, a tail there.

I reached over and the blast of crows sent me reeling back, gasping as a score of birds exploded into the air with a dozen mad screaming caws. Numb with surprise, my mouth open like a barn door, I was left staring at the rotten husk of a man half-devoured, dangling from a hemp noose squeezed tight around his busted neck.

What the crows had left of the putrid ripped flesh was leathery and tough, and the man's clothes sagged like melting tissue paper from the exposed bone and gristle.

My stomach didn't want to stay in place, and though the body's worst stench was likely passed, there was enough spoiled meat smell to send me into spasms. I've got a strong stomach, but there's few can hold on in such awful company as that flayed cadaver.

Funny, he wasn't much better to be around when he was alive.

"How you doing, Tony?" I whispered.

CHAPTER FOURTEEN

After that, I went back to the barn project, measuring out boards, marking, sawing, and pounding wood together with square-headed iron nails, saving some lumber back for the horse corral out front.

Time had taken its toll there too, and the gray rails begged to be replaced, the gates pining for new hinges.

Simple truth is, I'd been too much distracted by the vig life. Ranching is a never-ending string of chores. Farming is bad, too.

A man gets his window of opportunity to do a job, he better get it done. If he doesn't, the weather takes over or another job rears its head. Too much time riding for Cap Burnham's brand had put me underwater.

Too much time wandering the rough country revealed an ugly, hard truth.

By contrast, it was easy to separate warm red-cedar planks from vanilla pine, and simple work to stack them neat and tidy on one side of Betty's pen. Setting up a workspace there with a pair of narrow twin sawhorses and a rusty old toolbox had nothing to do with the complexities of crime or punishment.

I put up three new support posts to the ceiling and two new walls with studs fourteen inches apart.

For a while, my days made sense again.

In the old country, they would have cut notches and pegs when building a barn. They would have clamped seams together with ten times my precision. Some of the high plains pioneers still worked that way.

But not all of us. Under the guise of progress and innovation, the old ways were falling away fast. I liked the speed and efficiency of iron nails. Liked the hard, fast work of the hammer.

I worked fast to avoid the cold.

I worked hard to avoid thinking.

Mostly, I worked to forget the accusing stare of Tony Pike's rotting corpse and starve the gnawing desire for rum that every day made my bones feel hungry and vacant.

Every day felt like a month, but I didn't quit drinking for Ben Frymire or Cap Burnham.

God help me, I didn't even do it for Trudy, the gulf between us continuing on as wide as ever.

I didn't understand it then, but I did it for Tony — and all the Tony's yet to come.

For three weeks, I stayed dry inside and out.

Three weeks, I worked in the barn. A hundred years.

Naturally, Sonny was no help at all.

"Remember what Frymire said about them black-masked vigs? Ain't you gonna go back to looking for Kid Wade?"

After cutting Tony down from his oak tree grave, I gave him a more permanent resting spot in a shallow ditch along the banks of Plum Creek.

At first, I didn't tell anybody. Not even Trudy. Not until later.

"I've got my own life to lead, don't I?"

"I suppose you do."

Most days Sonny sat on Betty's milking stool or an upside-down pail to watch me work. He sipped from his bottomless flask, and it felt like the Devil was hovering at my neck tickling my cheek with a feather.

One day, he said, "Quick question, Gus. Are you still loyal to the Niobrara vigs? Just say yes or no."

"What kind of talk is that?"

"It's the kind of talk requires a straight answer."

"I told you before. I have my own life. Here, with Trudy. There's work to be done if we're going to make a go of it in the long haul."

He didn't believe me.

I spread my arms to encompass the debris of cut ends, sawdust, and tools at my feet. "If you've seen this mess and my answer isn't straight enough for you, I don't know what more I can say."

Sonny got up and followed me from one station to the next. Hovering over a pine two-by-four, tripping against me while I measured it, cut it, and carted it back to the framework taking shape.

"Can I tell you what I think?" he said.

"No."

"You're using all this work to avoid your problems."

"I lost a lot of time last month. Like Frymire said, chasing around the country, drinking too much. Trudy wants me to stay home."

"Yeah, well, that reads real nice for a flowery postcard, but it's just us men here, Gus."

I laid down my saw and pulled the pencil from behind my ear, tossed it down on the board I'd been fixing to cut.

"Meaning what?"

"Meaning you can't fool an old fool. You're worried sick about Albert. You mumble around here like broke-dick dog, picking at your food —"

"You're not my damned mother, and I've already got a wife."

"It don't take one of them matrons at church to see you and your wife ain't getting on so good either. Most young fellas your age can't stop frisking a woman with their eyes, and then get their hands busy lickety-split when the lights go out. The way you two steer clear of each other, it's like watching a pair of Catholic nuns."

"Go to hell, Sonny."

"That's another thing. There was a time you mighta said, by gosh, or by golly. But you're harder now. Working out here in the barn, every other word is hell, or damn, or shit on this thing or that person. I get tired of hearing that language. Them regulators used it a lot, too."

"That's a hell of an accusation — coming from you."

"Right there — see what I mean?"

I closed my eyes and tried to breathe, but it all got so overwhelming I fell back against Betty's stall and let the gate absorb my weight. The gentle cow took two steps forward and nosed my arm, snuffing loud, blowing hot air and bovine snot across the flannel sleeve of my shirt.

Sonny brought his shiny tin flask out from his back pocket, unscrewed the cap, and took a long drink. Ten feet away the pang of it quickened my heartbeat.

He offered the flask to me, but I willed my arms to be still.

"What do you expect me to do?" I said.

"I expect you to go find your friend before they vanish him, too."

Tony Pike's ghost rose up between us, and I squeezed my eyes shut.

I said, "And what if I do? What if I find him?"

Sonny was insistent. "Convince him to leave the country — for good this time. Or bring him in yourself and stay with him through the trial."

"Like a guard?"

"Like a friend watching out for him." Sonny took another long drink. "And find Shady Jane while you're at it. I got fifty dollars on her in a rematch with Manke's Miss Baghdad."

Outside, the sky was a solid gray pasteboard as night came on across the valley. Snowflakes etched their paths against the dark, chalk dust on a blackboard. A deceptive lantern glowed warm inside the house, and a wolf howled far in the distance. Behind me, Betty's reaction was a low rumbling moo of concern. Sonny took another long pull from his flask. I was starting to think he drank in front of me just because I'd turned him down and he enjoyed rubbing my face in it.

He capped the top and belched. "None of this ends until Albert's taken care of. Alive or dead, and you know how most everybody wants it."

"I'll go in the morning. I'll start to look again." I tried to sound convincing.

"That's a boy," Sonny said. "It's for Albert — but really it's for your own good."

"No," I said. "No, I don't think it is."

Because one of us was gonna end up in a coffin.

So I stayed home.

CHAPTER FIFTEEN

One day before Christmas, when the sun was directly overhead, a crummy six-wheeled wagon rolled into Pleasant Valley with a hill of cracked corn piled high in back, leaking through the cracks. The freighter on the bench was an African neighbor from the other side of Frymire's place. "How do, Ned?" I said.

"Doin' fine, Gus. Got some meal for your cows if you want it." He was the kind of man always helping out.

"Did you think we needed charity?" I had a sour tongue, not getting anywhere with my hunt for Albert. We only had Betty and one calf, plus the two horses, having sold off some stock to another neighbor named Hoffman. "But I'll take the load if your price is right."

We made a deal, and I asked Ned to back his wagon into the barn. Under a new set of ceiling braces we shoveled the corn into a grain closet I built. Sometimes a good sweat will do more than talking or ruminating or chewing on feelings. Shoulder to shoulder with Ned, I worked off my grump and showed off my handiwork in the barn.

Ned said, "Looks like you've been putting in some hours."

"Day and night," I said.

"Looks to be some good work."

"Thanks. I muddle along. Trial and error, you know how it is. You ever pick up a hammer?"

"My dad's a carpenter," he said. "So, yeah."

"Then you know."

We shook hands, and the hard calluses on his hands told the story. "I do know," he said.

After we settled up, Ned was fixed to leave, but Trudy wanted him to have some coffee and a sack of apple fritters. "She dries the apples in the fall and cuts them up fine," I said.

"Nothing like a good apple fritter."

While we waited, and just to make conversation, I said, "You ever hear from Timmons? He used to bring in a wagon of corn to us now and again."

Ned shook his head. "Never heard."

"We don't know much of anything up

here," I said. "Just what news you fellas bring us."

He offered a contagious smile and walked around the front wheel of his wagon and past the big hand brake, "It's your lucky day." Ned reached under the seat, pulled out a heavy canvas bag, and opened it. Inside was a stack of newspapers. He handed them over.

"I was going to use these for kindling, but you go ahead and keep 'em."

There must have been two or three months' worth of reading in the stack. "I thank you, Ned. You can pick them up next time you stop by."

"Naw, you get done with 'em, you use them yourself for your fire."

"Obliged," I said, flipping open the paper on top. It was the *Holt County Banner,* and what I read there nearly knocked me on my butt.

Kid Wade Shot

Rumor has it that Kid Wade was shot and killed by a man by name of Foster Richardson, en Plum Creek, while attempting to steal said Richardson's mules. Mr. Richardson is a hunter and trapper and follows it principally for a livelyhood, and supports

187

a fine span of mules, and we understand this was not the first attempt that had been made to steal his team, and he has been compelled to sleep by them for sometime past to keep them from vanishing. We suppose Kid, getting over anxious to secure such a valuable prize, made a bold attempt to do so, and recived [sic] his just dues in the form of a half ounce of lead backed by the force of a couple drams of powder, through his worhless [sic] body.
— *Holt County Banner,* December 6, 1883

"This can't be," I said, rolling my eyeballs over the print until the words smudged into an inky blur with the headline bleeding through clear as the stench of a rotting possum.

Kid Wade Shot.

It was the kind of finality to everything that had threatened to pull me down into the fog when I was heavy drinking. I hadn't had a drop of rum for a long time.

Plum Creek again.

I checked the date on the paper's masthead, December 6, and tried to read the copy one more time.

Ned's voice cut through the chatter in my head. "Something happen to somebody you know?"

188

I must've stared at him a second too long because his grin melted into a frown. Maybe I scared him. I can't imagine what my face looked like. I could hear my heart beat in my ears. Ned mounted his wagon and gave me a quick salute. Fingers clamped tight around Albert's death story, I ignored the other papers and they thumped to the ground, top layers flapping up like turkey vultures in the breeze, fluttering out fast across the yard. It was a clear day and the sheets of news were like gulls whipping across the Sandhills.

"You didn't let Ned leave without his fritters, did you?" Trudy asked, coming from the house with a curled-up sack and a glass jar of coffee sealed with a square of wax paper under the screw-top lid, sticking out on four sides. I pushed the paper under her nose. She dropped the jar but it didn't break.

Finally, she said, "Do you believe it?"

"I don't know what to believe."

"You remember Foster Richardson."

"Not particularly."

"He's got those mules on Plum Creek."

"That much I got from the story."

Trudy said, "He used to buy eggs from me."

Sonny waddled out from the direction of

the privy behind the house. "Who was that in the wagon?"

"Ned Witty."

"The paper says Albert's been killed," Trudy said.

"By the vigs?"

"By Foster Richardson," I said. "Over on Plum Creek."

"You fill a canteen, we'll ride over there right now. Find out what's what."

"I . . . don't think so," I said.

"You've been looking for Albert's tracks, here's something falls straight in your lap."

"I'll go by myself."

Trudy put her hand on my arm as the wind tossed her hair into a tangled swirl. "I'll go along with you."

After being together for so long, it was hard to see how neither Trudy nor Sonny knew enough to let me go. "You'd think you lived with a different man. The both of you," I scolded. "It's my job to track down Kid Wade, and by damn, I'll do it. Don't you see how you two would slow me down? If he is shot, he might be laying out there half-mad with fever, plugging lead balls into anything that comes near."

Which wasn't the thing to say, no matter how much I knew it likely wasn't true. Trudy's face showed ready horror, and Gus gripped my arm. He said, "All the more reason I back you up, son."

I shook him away and backed up a step. "You both stay here. I mean it. It's only a couple hours over to Plum Creek. I'll look up this Richardson and get his story. The clucking durn mud-hen is probably making it all up."

Sonny said, "Pitiful how people will lie to the paper with nothing more in mind than getting their name laid out by the typographer for their friends to see."

"It's the times we're living in."

"Take Richardson some fritters," Trudy said. "He might be more helpful if he thinks you're a friend."

I changed into a clean shirt not covered with grain dust and waited around long enough for Trudy to pack a lunch. Sonny gave in and walked Ed out to the yard for me, all saddled up. I was off to Plum Creek to claim a body or at least hear a fanciful story, maybe both, but as it turned out that evening, I never got the chance to get reacquainted with Foster Richardson.

At a quarter of one in the afternoon I hoofed out, and at four-thirty I followed a curly trail of dried cloverleaf into a glade of elm trees and maples on the west banks of Plum Creek about a quarter mile away from

Tony Pike's last remains.

Once down into a narrow cut in the road, I saw the curve of a hoofprint in the dry mud. A hunch ushered me along the edge of the trees and broken stems of grass and a tuft of horsehair on some tree bark coaxed me to keep moving. Winter dark had settled across the sky with one bright pinpoint of light at the horizon when I finally smelled woodsmoke.

I climbed down from the saddle and wrapped Ed's reins around a tree branch. Giving his neck an appreciative slap, I ducked under a pine branch, letting my nose sniff its way forward until I made out yellow-orange tongues of flame wagging at me through the branches.

The fire taunted me, and reacting from emotion was a big part of my problem, back then. It's what put me in Dutch with Trudy and probably the vigs like Frymire who figured me for a drunk — turns out he wasn't alone in that judgment — and bulling straight ahead without thinking is what got me ambushed by Kid Wade.

CHAPTER SIXTEEN

I'd been hunting for Albert all these weeks. Could this be his campfire?

I jerked away a cedar bough to find out.

Behind me, a twig snapped on the forest floor.

Spinning around I saw what was coming and had no defense.

Albert stepped forward, and his punch was like the kick of a Missouri mule. I staggered back into the knobby trunk of a hundred-year-old elm.

I levered myself up to puff out my chest.

If me and Albert were gonna play like banty cocks lookin' to dig spurs into one another, I reckoned I could give as good as I got.

I stomped up to him so fast, Albert didn't have time to react. "You wanna have a go, let's have a go." I moved him three paces toward a sprawling tall cedar with a powerful shove.

Albert poked out his bottom lip and nodded. "Suits me fine. This oughtn't take too long."

I was plenty riled up, a boiling mixture of relief and humiliation. Glad that Albert appeared whole and uninjured. Sore that he'd ambush me in the near dark of night.

Foster Richardson's story was nothing more than a whopper of a fish story filling space until the day the paper wrapped a stream-caught rainbow trout. Damned if it wasn't all the *Banner* was good for.

"What are you waiting for, Kid?"

Albert Wade was never a good-looking boy, but what his squat legs and thin shoulders lost in size, his agility and quick reflexes made up for with elegance, though you'd never know it looking at his clumsy posture. His face was forever half smudged with a charcoal coat of whiskers that sprang back only seconds after the shaving. And his ears were too big, his eyebrows too heavy.

In the light of his flickering campfire, he was like an elf in one of those old Grimms' fairy stories, or the troll who hides in the dark and the shadows under a bridge.

For a long time, me and the other Pony Boys lived in his aura of black magic, his conjurings of clever rationalizations and word games, his confused sense of right and wrong. Always clowning, with every utterance having more than one meaning, he kept us entertained and encouraged.

With Kid Wade, everything was possible. He was a court jester who, for a while, made me see life through his mad lens, believing in the ghosts and charms and spooks he called *booses*. Thinking back, I was all the better for it — and all the worse.

He circled out around me toward the elm tree, deeper under the shadow of its fat branches.

Patches of dirty snow still lingered at the north and southbound roots, and crusts of ice nested between dormant tall weeds, damp and exposed.

Just the way I felt. Damp and exposed.

Albert said, "If it isn't my old pal, August John. The way I heard it, you're in so tight with Cap Burnham's regulators, a fart don't fit between you boys. Is that right?"

"I've got nothing to be ashamed of."

"You never did. Leastways, not that you'd admit."

The accusation set my teeth on edge. Not to mention, I had a sore jaw where Albert had poked me. I worried the tender spot inside my cheek where my teeth had scraped flesh. Albert had a heck of a wallop.

"C'mon then," I said, "ya damned sheep-herder."

It was the insult he'd always used on us — half joking, half serious. He took it the same way.

With a loud, joyous cackle, he ran at me, head down, arms wide. If he got me on the ground, I was through. Nobody outwrestled Kid Wade.

Rather than wait to be tackled, I timed a fast lunge to the right, leaving my left leg in place for Al to trip over. He stumbled, not without bruising my shin, and windmilled fifteen feet toward the campfire before regaining his balance on the slippery ground.

By then, I was on him and managed to pay him back for my jaw with an open-handed slap. I rocked his stubborn lead skull from one side to the other without any noticeable effect.

"You still hit like a Sunday school teacher," he said.

Then he cranked a balled-up fist under my ribs, blasting the breath from me. I scrabbled backwards to put distance be-tween us, struggled to inhale. He was a good scrapper. Ruthless and mean. I was always too hesitant, afraid I'd hurt somebody beyond repair.

I held up my bruised hands, urging him to slow up. "We both got some licks in. How about you hear me out?"

"Not hardly."

"Yeah," I said, reading him like I always could. "I 'spect this is the way it's got to be."

"Long as you're playing turncoat."

"Turncoat against what? Against you?"

He continued to circle, keeping me off balance. "Maybe against yourself."

"Hell, I ain't the man I once was," I said. "Too many years have gone past. You ain't who you once were either." He didn't say anything, just kept his flat eyes hooded under his hat. I pressed on. "You came to Pleasant Valley once and told me we were quits. You remember? All them years ago, before they hauled you off to jail. You said, me and you were done."

"You got nothing I want," he confirmed.

"It ain't always about you. Maybe it's what I want. What Trudy wants."

Using Trudy's name caught him off guard, and I took the opportunity to punch him in the nose. He caterwauled like a scalded hog and I hit him again in the same spot, drawing a rush of blood. He went down to one knee, and I stood above him. "You give yourself up to me, I promise to stand with you."

Hands cupping his face, he made like he was going to spring up at me, and I kicked the side of his head like a watermelon. It thumped with a hollow, pleasing sound and he rolled over on his back in the dirt.

I resisted the urge to stomp his groin, but not the urge to crow a little. "You deserve a real beating, you know that? I'd love nothing more than to thrash the stuffing out of you for the next couple hours."

"Bastard," he mewled.

"That's you, not me."

"Pissant sonuvabitch."

"Rock head."

"Dog breath."

"Mud for brains."

Ugly as he was, he grinned easily. "You are."

I couldn't think of anything. "Stinkin' stinky . . . stink."

"Dog breath."

"You already said that."

Through the tears and the blood and the anger, he laughed.

"Booger face," I said.

"Whore bait."

I reached for his hand, and he clasped my arm, pulled himself up.

Then he hit me in the guts again, and I doubled over.

"Stupid as a sheepherder," he said.

After a few seconds, I straightened up. Albert raised his hands in surrender, cocked his head back toward the fire. "I got a cup of coffee over there. Truce?"

He put out his hand.

I ignored it and walked toward the fire. "Truce," I said.

CHAPTER SEVENTEEN

We sat with the fire between us, feeding it long blades of grass and brush, tossing in bits of dry wood and sticks, rubbing our sores, enduring the cuts and bruises decorating both our frames but hiding the pain from each other in shadows cast by the fire.

"Your coffee's burned," I said.

"You don't have to drink it." He leaned back on a toppled length of cedar, and slurped with greed, swishing the liquid around inside his cheeks before spitting it out. "I got to tell you, Gus. I already got the message. You didn't have to tramp all the way out here to tell me."

"What message?"

Albert guffawed good and loud and started to cough. "You're teasing me," he said, sputtering for breath. After the theatrics, he pitched the coffee grounds from his cup and pulled a plug of wet, wrapped leaf tobacco from his coat pocket. He held it up to me. "You want a chaw?"

I patted the cigarette makings in my shirt pocket. "Got my own," I said.

"Don't let me stop you." His jagged yellow teeth cut a healthy chunk from the corner of the plug, and he jammed it back into his pocket. Next, he pulled out a short length of rope, maybe eight inches long. He liked to practice tying knots.

While I rolled a smoke, Albert put his left boot up to the fire and kicked at a half-baked roll of oak. "Like I said, I got your message plenty clear. I heard about Billy Morris. And Culbertson. Heard how you beat down Baron Hale and torched his house for feeding me a tater."

"He had it coming."

"Yeah, that was some good tater. Don't blame you for being pissy about it." Albert held up his cup. "Guess you're guilty now too. We've shared coffee and a smoke. You gonna turn yourself in for a skull cracking? I figure Ted Roberts would be all too happy to oblige you."

"You're coming back with me."

"And end up vanished? No, sir."

"Baron Hale is back with his family."

"That's not what I heard."

Again, Tony's ghost snuggled up to me, but I pressed on. "Has it occurred to you

201

there's a lot you might hear that's not true?"

Albert snickered. "I'm pretty good at smelling horse apples."

"I thought I was too, but let me tell you why I came up here."

"Because of Foster Richardson's mules." He held up his rope, showed me the taut-line hitch he'd put around a twig. "Am I right? You read the newspaper?"

I finished making my cigarette and picked up a smoldering elm twig, touched the glowing ember. "You're supposed to be dead," I said.

"After three days, I rose again."

"Trudy would beat your behind for that kind of blasphemy."

"She always was the Bible reader."

In his own way, he meant it as a compliment, but it rubbed me a little raw.

Albert stretched out his jacket and poked three fingers through a trio of adjacent holes. "Richardson took a few shots at me." He wiggled his middle finger. "This one here scraped the inside of my beltline."

"Word is you were after his mules."

"You look around here before you go. See if you find a single, solitary mule." He unraveled his knot and put together another. This time he worked on a timber hitch.

"How about Frymire's Kentucky mare?

Will I find Shady Jane?"

"Jane gone missing, has she?"

"Like you don't know."

Albert leaned back to enjoy his chewing tobacco.

Finally, he said, "You remember that day at Virgil Manke's race, you and me watching Frymire brush ol' Jane down?"

"I remember. Never saw a coat so fine, like cake frosting, and her black legs and mane like sweet licorice."

"We weren't the only ones giving that mare the covetous eyeball."

"Who do you mean?"

"I honestly didn't know she was missing." He spit a long stream of tobacco juice into the dirt and it pooled up beside the fire. "What you gotta understand is that if I knew who had her, I still wouldn't tell you. That's the way of most everybody up here on this cursed river now. Nobody's got a damned thing to say."

"Half the county's mixed up in your mischief."

"Folks don't want to go missing." The vigs were obviously sitting at the front of his mind.

"If these, ah . . . folks, have nothing to hide, they shouldn't be afraid to say something."

Albert wagged his head. "How can you sit there, a grown man — but talk so green?"

"You remember Timmons, the man who used to haul freight in for us?"

Albert said he did.

"Trudy said he's vanished. She used that exact word."

"It's happened to more than one person," Albert said. His voice was mocking and sarcastic then. "Like you don't know."

"I guess I don't."

Albert said, "Well, I guess I don't know about Shady Jane."

"You hear anything from your dad?"

So far, Albert acted like he hadn't heard about his stepdad. I was going to tell him, see what reaction I could get, maybe ferret out some information. But at the last minute, I decided not to go in that direction. I wanted to protect his feelings.

It's what I told myself.

"I don't have a dad," Albert said. Then he looked at me with what I would've called concern in any other person. Almost a real expression of caring. "You don't either, Gus."

"I know it," I said. My dad had died many years before. It was common knowledge.

"It ain't what I mean. What I'm talking about is Cap Burnham. Or Manke. Or

Sonny Clausen. These ol' boys ain't your dad. You got nothing to prove to them. You're twice the man of any of them." He undid his piece of rope and jammed it into his pocket.

I wasn't sure how it made me feel to hear him say such a thing. It was unlike him to be so complimentary, especially when, less than an hour before, he'd been trying to stomp my ribs. But it was just like him, too. He was never one to hold in what he felt. Never somebody to shy away from what he wanted to say.

"My advice is to get out now, Gus. You and Trudy live your own life. You leave the vigs to tend to themselves."

"Turns out, it's your old man got me into it to start with."

"And I got a hunch Trudy's told you to leave it alone. Same as me."

"She has."

"Do me a favor," he said. "Take her advice."

"Or what?"

He shut down then, and his look was inscrutable — meaning I wouldn't be able to tell what he meant if I spent another three hours with him. And I was the one knew him the best, which I think is true, even more than Eph Weatherwax who many said was his first lieutenant and best friend. We never talked about Eph, the two of us.

I repeated the question, "Or what?"

"You give my best to Trudy when you see her," he said.

"Come with me and see her for yourself."

"She changed much the last few years?"

"Naw. Like you said, reading her Bible. Worrying over that damn mutt, McGee."

"Same old Trudy."

"She's got a few more freckles. The summers have been awful hot, and she works too hard. Needs a new sunbonnet."

"That sounds like her."

"Why not come home with me?"

"Get stuffed."

"Anyway, we're back where we started. With everybody looking for you, how far do you think you'll get?"

"I dunno," he said. "Figured I'd mosey on back to Iowa, one of these days. Got some people over there I know who've got a farm. Good people called Mansfield."

A footstep came from the woods beyond our camp, followed by another.

We both turned to see Sonny Clausen duck in from under a tree, fire gleaming on his outstretched carbine. "Time to go home, Albert."

He was drunk.

Albert turned on me with the fury of a coiled-up rattlesnake. "Shoulda figured you'd have your sidekick along. Everything set up in your favor, eh Gus?"

"I didn't — I told Sonny to stay home." I climbed to my feet, cursing. "This isn't my doing."

Sonny took another few steps forward, the barrel of his rifle level with Albert's chin. "I won't tell you again, Kid. You get your boots underneath you and start walking."

I said, "Nobody's going anyplace until you lower that gun."

"Told you before, Gus. This don't end until Kid Wade is taken care of, alive or dead. It makes no difference to me."

"Put the gun down."

"Oh, for cryin' out loud," Albert said, and he scooped up a cup full of sparking red embers and tossed them in Sonny's face.

"Gaa-aah!"

As Sonny flew backwards, his rifle went off with an ear-deafening boom, and I made a lunge for Albert. But I was too slow, just nicking the hem of his jacket as he scurried away toward the woods.

"Aw, Sonny!" I spun back around to find the old man rolling back and forth in the leafy underbrush, clutching his bleeding head where he'd struck it on a rock. "You big idiot."

I knelt beside him, trying to inspect his wound.

"Naw, no," he said, slapping at my hands. "Go get 'im. Go get the Kid."

"It's too late for that. He's gone. You've scared him off."

"Aww, God, Gus. I'm sorry." He sobbed like a kid, smearing blood across his face as he wiped at his tears. Rolling over and over in the dirt, he cried. "I'm sorry. I'm so sorry."

"I know you are, Sonny."

To this day, I wonder how things would have turned out, had I gone after him. Maybe I would've caught up with him. Maybe he wouldn't have gone to Iowa, and maybe me and Biff and Ted Roberts wouldn't have gone after him with C.C. Dodge.

Maybe is a word filled with regrets.

On Christmas Eve, Trudy made oyster soup for me and Sonny with milk and butter and salt. The oysters floated around like little black treasures in our steaming bowls, and we split 'em even steven. I sopped up my helping with homemade wheat bread, but there was still some left in the big pot. Before Trudy read the nativity story, I carried what remained in the pot to the door, and opened it onto the crisp, starry night. Planning to set the leftovers out for the cats, I almost tripped on a paperboard box with a red ribbon tied around it.

I carried it inside to the table.

"What is it?"

"It's addressed to you."

Sonny and I watched as Trudy untied the ribbon and folded open the top. She reached inside, and gently removed a brand-new sunbonnet.

"Oh, Gus, it's lovely."

I waited a few days before telling her it wasn't from me.

CHAPTER EIGHTEEN

The new year started fresh, as every other year with Trudy had, by taking a complete inventory of our cupboards. I believed her habit of taking stock was a good one, and I encouraged the project every year. With 1884 underway, it was good to know where we stood. Not only was it something we could do together inside, away from the wind and cold, it made the difference between living through a Nebraska winter and barely surviving. It still does, I guess.

"Beans?" I said.

"Check," she said.

"Coffee."

"Nope."

"How much lye is on hand for soap?"

"Not enough."

My job was to sit at the round table and think up as many of our daily needs as I could. Trudy counted items on the shelves and in her pie safe next to the stove. We had storage in the back room too, as well as outside in the barn. Once we finished in the house, we'd go there and check on the animals, too.

I marked my paper list with a pencil, adding goods as Trudy remembered them. "We should see if Tarbell has some India ink. Maybe a color other than black."

"Red?"

"Put it on the list."

The first clear day in January we bundled up and left with the sun for the store at Carns. Tarbell kept a wagon going twice a month back and forth to the railroad in Long Pine, and if we left Pleasant Valley early, we were sure to get back from Carns shortly after dark. I considered leaving Sonny at home to do the chores. I told him, "If a snowstorm blows up, somebody's got to be here to feed and water the animals."

"Ain't no snow gonna blow up, August John," he said. "My knees do a fine job of forecasting the weather. They're telling me we're in for a dry spell. Besides, I got needs of my own."

Which meant he was low on rum.

I didn't argue.

After making sure all was secure, we hitched up Levi and followed the trail south, pulling into Carns in the forenoon. I parked the wagon in front of Tarbell's store.

The burly storekeeper stepped out to greet me in front of the hand-painted sign next to the door: Square Man, Square Deals — a local joke as Tarbell was as wide as he was tall. A living five by five. When he shook my hand, it felt like I was affixed to an anchor. "Some of your boys are inside," he said, his cheeks lifting in a gap-toothed grin.

I recognized Cap Burnham's horse at the hitching rail, and while I helped Sonny down from the wagon, Ted Roberts rode up wearing his top hat.

Tarbell said, "Hi, Ted."

Ted ignored the fat man, and addressed me instead. "Well, if it ain't a stranger, I don't know one. Howdy, stranger."

"Howdy, Ted. How's everything?"

"Can't complain." He offered Trudy and Sonny a greeting, then invited me into the store behind Tarbell. "I was just gonna share a drink with Cap. How about joining us?"

"I think I've got a job already lined up," I said, watching Trudy's expression. "I'm here to carry boxes."

Before Ted could say anything, Sonny spoke up and answered for me, like he was my conscience or something.

"You go on ahead, August John. I'll help Trudy collect what she needs."

Tarbell was behind his counter now and agreed. "We can take care of the packages," he said. "You go on and visit with your pals."

I didn't see as I had much choice. I wasn't overly keen to insert myself back into the regulators' plans. But, on the other hand, I wasn't about to be rude to men who had done no wrong to me personally. There was no need to get on their bad side, that's for sure.

"Why not," I said. "Lead the way."

His face was as full of dirty pink pimples as ever.

Ted pushed his spectacles up his nose, then slapped me on the back. "We've had some adventures lately, let me tell you. Boy, you're missing out."

That's not the way it sounded when Cap told it.

"It was a nightmare," Cap said, storming around the room while Ted and I sat at the same table where, only a month before, I pounded the daylights out of Baron Hale. "The wedding and the bawling bride and the mother of the groom grabbing at my shirt cuffs. And then this business with William Freese. By god, Gus, we've got egg on our faces, sure!"

For my benefit, Ted said, "It ain't as bad

as all that. We brought back sixteen stole horses."

Cap slammed one of the stools back against the wall and shook a finger at him. "A nightmare," he said. "We've lost three months' goodwill with the settlers in the space of one week."

"We scooped up a dozen bad men, and he calls it a nightmare," Ted said.

Cap fired back, "If folks ain't on our side, we're through."

Ted rolled his eyes.

The way Cap told it, he, Ted, and Virgil Manke had trekked cross-country to Niobrara City right after Christmas on a tip that the Cline Brothers were holed up south of town at their ranch with Eph Weatherwax, his pa, a couple Beltezore cousins, and possibly Kid Wade. After a chilly ride, what they discovered, when they rode up to Judge Cooley's office, was the tail end of a wedding for one of the Clines and the sixteen-year-old virginal waif, Mary Berry.

"Mr. and Mrs. Cline were coming out as we were going in," Cap said. "So first thing you know, bean brain here pulls iron and pries the two lovers apart."

"I'd recognize that polecat even without the rapture of marital bliss pasted all over his face."

"He means lipstick," Cap said.

"So I arrested Cline right then and there."

"In front of God, Judge Cooley, and half the town."

Imagine how the hysterical new bride must've felt as her husband was hauled away in irons. It was a bizarre occurrence to be sure. "The couple didn't take too kindly to the interruption? I can't figure why."

My sarcasm went over Ted's knobby head. "It sure wasn't worth the histrionics that went on. Cline was on his knees begging me to let him spend his wedding night with his new wife in the room next door to ours."

"You two held this fellow overnight? Next door to his bride?"

"He literally begged to go see her. Ain't that a laugh?"

Judging from the look on Cap's face, it became less laughable by the second, so I asked him, "Who's this Freese you mentioned?"

"German farmer. Big shot up there with a lot of money. That's another damn thing."

Ted stood up and walked to the door. "I've heard this story before," he said. "Anybody need a fresh drink?" Cap and I both had cups half full of coffee, so we told him no.

After Ted left the room, Cap pointed in

the direction Ted went.

"That one thinks he's God almighty out there."

"As bad as that?"

"Worse. You shoulda seen Ted with poor Cline. When he says the man was begging, it's no exaggeration. Ted reveled in kicking mud in the sorry groom's face."

"Tell me about this German farmer, Freese."

I could see Cap was sincere when he said, "I swear. Gus, my information came straight from Virgil Manke, and he got it from an eyewitness. Freese has a place three miles outside Niobrara, and Kid Wade's been living there with him the last two months."

"All these leads on the Kid, yet none of them panned out."

"The little runt is always one step ahead of us." Cap's eyebrows rode high on his forehead. "I believe he was with Freese."

"Just not when you arrested him."

"We had the old kraut in hand, Ted was sweating him — not too hard — when Judge Cooley shows up with twenty of the same busybodies saw us arrest Cline after his wedding."

"You already had the public against you."

Cap started counting the old man's blessings. "William Freese is a member of the

Masonic and Oddfellow Societies. He's a member of Niobrara's Grand Army Post. He's got more money than King Solomon."

"So at least two things most folks don't have," I said. "A lot of money and a lot of status."

"Either one will buy you out of the noose. Both things together made Manke, Ted, and me look like donkeys." He walked over to a bookshelf and picked up a folded copy of the newspaper.

"Read it for yourself," he said, pitching the paper in my direction.

Mr. F says he purchased the horses in good faith and is perfectly willing to undergo a rigid, searching investigation in regard to all the facts and circumstances in the case. It will require the best kind of evidence, something more than the confession of thieves, to convince the people of Niobrara that Mr. Freese is anything but what he always appeared to be, one of our best citizens.

The vigilantes are doing good service in hunting down this infamous gang of thieves that has been a terror to farmers in Knox, Holt and Brown Counties, and should be aided and assisted by every honest citizen in the land. That mistakes will be made and the reputation of innocent men temporarily clouded, is to be expected, but the ultimate result will be for the benefit of the community.

— *Holt County Banner,* December 1883

"You got some good comments here at the end," I said.

"Not good enough. Sure we corralled some renegades and shuffled them down to O'Neill to stand trial. But when we pulled out of Niobrara, our tails were between our legs."

"What you need is a solid win. Something the people can't dispute."

"What we need is the Kid."

Ted Roberts said, "I agree." Neither Cap nor I had noticed him standing at the edge of the door, holding a full brown bottle with a tight grip around the neck.

I didn't like his tone of voice.

"I agree," he said again. "We absolutely need the Kid. How about you tell us where we can find him, Gus?"

"Me? How would I know?"

Ted scoffed, and I felt my guts turn to water. "Maybe you'd know because he told you where he was going when you cozied up to him at Plum Creek. Maybe because you're no different than Freese or Baron

Hale or any of these pathetic sodbusters. Aiding and abetting, Gus — it'll get you hanged in our neck of the woods."

Dammit, Sonny!

I knew I should've left the old blabbermouth home.

The room was still as the grave, and Ted's steps were a resounding death knell. He pulled out the chair next to me and sat down hard.

Cap Burnham's breath came as if through the hot, flared nostrils of a bull, loud and gearing up to charge. I needed to pull everybody away from the ledge we were about to go over.

"First off, I don't know what Sonny told you."

Ted held his jaw rigid. He looked twenty years older than he was. "You and Albert Wade. Plum Creek. Nattering away like schoolgirls."

There was no use in denying it. "I found his camp. I tried to convince him to come in."

"You gave him a choice?"

"I was determined to bring him in," I said. Which had the benefit of being the truth.

Cap's voice was a lot less incriminating than Ted's. "Why'd you let him go, Gus?"

"I didn't *let* him go. He *got away.* Two

different things."

"Tell us what happened."

I did my best to reconstruct the circumstances leading up to the evening at Plum Creek. I told them about Frymire's and Biff Barlow's visit — about Frymire quitting the Association. I told them about searching for Kid and Shady Jane, about my wanderings in the rough country along the Keya Paha and the tributaries of the Running Water, carefully leaving out the facts surrounding my grisly reunion with Tony Pike.

Finally, I told them about Sonny's surprise intrusion at the Kid's campfire and hot coals flying into the old man's face.

I slammed Ted with a question of my own. "I don't suppose Sonny related to you how it's his own damn fault Albert bolted away?"

All too conveniently, Ted changed the subject. "Sonny told me Albert left a Happy Christmas package on your doorstep."

"He left it for Trudy. She's his cousin."

Cap asked, "How long ago'd this package show up?"

"Ted's got it right. It was at Christmas."

"So Albert could be anywhere by now."

Seeing another chance to step in, Ted said, "Sonny heard Albert say he was going to Mansfield's farm near Le Mars, Iowa. Ain't that true, Gus? Don't tell me it isn't."

220

He threatened with the bottle of hootch like he'd break my skull if I disagreed.

"I won't deny that's what Albert told me."

Cap sighed long and loud. Finally, he let his eyes travel back and forth between us and said, "It's your foul-up, Gus. You need to make things right or there's going to be trouble between us."

I couldn't stand the self-satisfied way Ted Roberts leaned back in his chair, looking down through his jar-bottom glasses at me. He clucked his tongue. "I never would have expected it from you, Gus."

Cap said, "That's enough, Ted." Then he turned back to me. "The truth is, Albert will let you get closer than me or Manke. I'd like to give you a second chance. When do you want to go get him?"

Ted took a big drink and slammed the bottle to the table. "Right now."

Cap kept his eyes on me. "Gus?"

"I've got barn construction to finish."

For the first time, Cap's voice held a threat over my head. Nothing explicit was said, but the tone was clear. "Maybe I'm not being clear. You've got unfinished business here to take care of first."

I sure enough felt like the biggest heel in the world sitting there in front of Cap — and I never wanted to shove a man's lips straight down his gullet more than right then with Ted Roberts. But the truth was, there was nothing Cap could say or do to lose my respect. He'd always played straight with me, even if I'd sinned against him by omission.

Ted Roberts could dry up and blow away, but I owed Burnham. "Give me a couple days," I said. "Let me take Frymire and Barlow."

"From what you said, are you sure Ben will go with you?"

"If there's a good chance of finding Shady Jane, he'll go. I'll convince him to go. They're both good men, and I trust 'em."

"Barlow hasn't always been so trustworthy."

"As far as I know, Albert doesn't know Biff. He won't recognize him."

Cap nodded. "You take Ted with you."

"Damn right," Ted said.

"Somebody to watch over me?" I said to Cap.

Ted spoke up. "Somebody to put a bullet in you if you don't behave."

CHAPTER NINETEEN

In the end, Frymire wouldn't go along with me and Biff and Ted to Iowa. "I told you, Gus — I'm quits. You find Shady Jane, you let me know. Otherwise, I'm done."

I think he was afraid we might take a side road on the way back and hang Kid Wade from a tall oak tree. In fact, I'm sure he believed it even though I explained to him that kind of unlawful act was what I was going along to prevent.

But he wouldn't hear it.

Trudy understood, though she wasn't jumping for joy. Sonny was ecstatic and darned near in the saddle before I could forbid him from coming along. His yapping drunk tongue was the last thing we needed along for the ride. Sonny wasn't the least bit sorry for running off at the mouth to Ted.

And at the last minute, Cap asked C.C. Dodge of the Chelsea regulators to drive a wagon for us with two gray geldings. We had been packed up with provisions on three horses, ready to set out when Dodge showed up with the open buckboard. "Mind if I tag along?"

Well, why not?

Dodge was the definition of the tall, laconic cowboy — not unlike Frymire — and his mouth chewed his wooden Lucifer matches easily, working them down to nubs. "Tryin' to quit with the 'backy," but he smoked a pipe.

Between the two of them, Burnham and Dodge agreed that once we had Albert in custody, we should transport him straight to one of those famous *undisclosed locations,* there being complaints out for him all over the country.

Cap said, "We need to do everything we can to forestall a neck-tyin' party until we can figure things out."

"Holt County wants him awfully bad," I said.

"So does Yankton. So does Wyoming. I'm not about to turn him over to strangers. This is our business to clean up."

But Cap was sorta vague on the details. There was nothing to do but go along and mind my manners.

I made sure I had plenty of fixings to roll

a smoke whenever I might need one. Dodge had a fifty-dollar contribution from a friend of his named Lamoureaux. "For food and shelter." We were well enough situated to leave for what was then called the Broken Kettle country of Iowa because of all the busted Indian crocks along Broken Kettle Creek, a tributary of the Big Sioux River.

Eventually the *Yankton Press* described the four of us riders, Dodge, me, Ted, and Biff, as "rough-looking men . . . heavily armed," and I guess you could say it's true. Nobody from Nebraska looks their best in the frozen heart of winter, and our overcoats and sweaters liked to bristle with guns.

Dodge rode with a Peacemaker on the hip and a Springfield .50-.70 trapdoor rifle beside him, and Ted Roberts carried a mean short-barreled scattergun. Flanking the wagon's left side atop Ed, I wore my old double-action Colt .41 at the hip and left my Frontier pistol at home for Trudy. My gun was nicknamed "The Thunderer," and it was a weapon Albert had long coveted. Back in our days as Pony Boys, he had the same model, but chambered for a .38 cartridge. That gun was known to gun enthusiasts as "The Lightning."

Albert wanted to own both models, telling me he'd "bring the storm." Thunder and lightning, see? He was jealous of my gun a long time.

An old pimp I knew once named Heavy Frahm said chums is the worst kind of jealous.

The worst kind of enemies.

I still had my Colt but what with being in prison all those years, I figured Albert traded his long ago. He was fickle like that. Looking back, I took the Thunderer along to Le Mars just to pester him.

Opposite me on a dashing palomino, Biff Barlow had a ball counting up the miles. Having done penance with Frymire working on some cattle together, the two had become close friends, and Barlow had changed his ways. He was reformed and by now I considered him as good a neighbor as any. He sat upright in the saddle, his big belly loving the saddle horn, his mount trotting along like she thought we were cavalry men advancing into uniformed battle. Most of the way across Nebraska and over the Missouri to Iowa, Biff kept a goofy expression of wonder and surprise plastered to his pink jowls.

He was just so damn pleased to come along with us. We were men, doing important things. I recognized the feeling.

I tried to share in it.

226

We stayed over that first night in Paddock at a hotel and saloon called Humpy's. I was there years before when it was little more than a hole in the ground, and it was still going strong. There was a new piano in the corner, and bearded Humpy dished out piles of chicken gizzards with onions and enough grease to keep your food chute polished. We washed everything down with warm beer and slept like kings. I wondered if Mr. Lamoureaux's contribution would hold out?

Early the next morning, we kept going.

Dodge was our navigator, plotting a commonsense tour along the Running Water up to the Niobrara, across the Missouri to Vermillion and then east to Le Mars, once called St. Paul Junction, on the Floyd River, named after Lewis and Clark's Sergeant Floyd.

The landscape in Knox County buckled in long, sloping hills with more tree lines and short horizons. The gray clouds formed like lye soap in the January sky above, and every so often a few lazy flakes somersaulted down, landing soft in horsehair or on our cheeks. Nobody thought twice about a storm. Nobody worried about it. Back then we could smell a squall coming. Or feel it in our joints.

Somewhere around Pishelville, C.C. Dodge got Ted Roberts picking up bones.

It was a harmless diversion at first, starting with the kind of idle chatter gents make bouncing along on the spring seat next to one another over the rolling prairie.

"We get to Yankton, I'll introduce you a Santee Indian I know who's looking for old bones. Trades 'em with young fellars like you for a roll with his daughter." Dodge held up a solemn hand. "Honest, son. She goes by the name of Pink Blossom."

The whole idea sounded great to Ted. Eagerly, he asked, "What am I looking for?"

Dodge cooked up a story on the spot. "Ancient elephants, monsters, horses — well, like that one there." He pointed at a white spot in the brown grass. Ted leaned far out over the wagon wheel to inspect the indicated spot on the prairie.

"Reckon that's a remnant from one of them ancient monsters?" Ted said.

Dodge urged him along, sliding his match from one corner of his mouth to the other. "Sure enough. You go down and get it."

Caught up in the endeavor, Ted leaped up from his seat and jumped off the moving wagon. I watched him run over and kick at the half-submerged bone until it was free. Caked in mud, he carried it along beside me, brushing chunks of sod and grass away with a gloved hand.

"Looks kinda like a pelvis bone, don't it, Gus?" Ted held the artifact up for me to see.

"Might be a pelvis at that."

"Maybe one of them Indian lion-men?"

"Maybe a coyote," Biff said.

Dodge couldn't keep the humor out of his voice. "Ooh, I 'spect it's something more exotic than a coyote." He cleared his throat, trying to keep a straight face. "I think it's a lion-man, sure."

"Do you really think so?" Ted ran up to the wagon and caught the iron handle near the brake lever. He hoisted himself back up to the bench.

Dodge pulled an empty burlap sack from under his seat. "How about you put it in here."

Ted stashed away his prize.

"You keep an eye open, and I'll slow up if we see any more." He glanced over at me and winked, sharing his glee at the trick he was pulling on Ted.

It was harmless fun, but I wondered how Ted would react when he found out the old Santee didn't have any need for a sack of three-dozen cow bones and "Pink Blossom" turned out to be an old grandma.

Ted didn't have much of a sense of humor.

As the miles wore on, Biff started whistling a medley of church music. Every time he got a third of the way along, I thought I recognized the tune — but then things went south. Pretty soon, I stopped listening, but Mr. Dodge would sometimes hum along. We weren't riding so close to have much conversation.

Every so often, Ted would rough me up with an accusing squint or cute remark like he expected me to scamper away to my outlaw hidey-hole at any turn. Whenever he looked, I gave him a casual nod, but he didn't have much to say. It was hard to keep from laughing at the bone sack he kept rattling along on his lap.

By Yankton, Ted carried around forty pounds of assorted bleached remains — and what kind of wild skeleton we might've built from the stuff he'd picked up off the prairie! Vermillion came and went before the truth dawned on him.

"There ain't no Santee man who collects bones, is there?"

Biff couldn't hold back with the giggles.

Dodge was sober as a nun on Good Friday. "Why do you say that, Ted?"

"I been cartin' these bones for nigh on forever, and we're well past Yankton."

"You just hold tight, Ted. Them bones will come in mighty handy any time now."

With Biff snickering, and Dodge pulling a long face, I busted out with a laugh. It was all just so ridiculous. Ted's face impersonated the sunset behind us, going from pink to red to purple, and he used a string of oaths I had never heard.

"Aw, heck," Dodge said, "we were just having some fun with you. Gotta pass the time somehow. Next time, I'll pick on Gus over there, what do you say?"

Which was as close as Ted was going to get by way of apology from Dodge.

From me, he'd get even less.

Ted dumped the sack of bones overboard with a clatter, then moved to the wagon box to ride, moping all the way into Le Mars where we stayed overnight at the hotel.

I didn't like the kid, but I had hoped he was more grown up.

I was wrong.

CHAPTER TWENTY

We were gathered together on the boardwalk in front of the Le Mars Farmers' Livery Stable with a man named Slim Reynolds. His brother, Don, stood so close to his side it reminded me of those Bunker twins from Siam forever joined at the hip I read about. I didn't think either one of the Reynolds boys would know what I was talking about if I said they looked like Chang and Eng Bunker. Heck, the Reynolds twins didn't know Nebraska from Nantucket Island. Or coal lumps from lemon drops.

Born on a dusty claim outside town, the identical brothers had never traveled more than twenty miles in any direction, something they both bragged about to us four strangers fresh in their town.

And a pleasant little town it was. The progressive street in front of the barn smelled clean with new paint, and at least two boys were busy mucking out stalls, carting wheelbarrows of mostly straw in and out of the interior stables. Slim and Don ran a tidy place.

The Reynoldses' pa was a city father, and their ma was famous. Slim explained, "Le Mars is named for six women who settled in the area and submitted their names as an acronym. Lucy Underhill, Elizabeth Parson, Mary Weare — that's my second-cousin on my dad's side, Anna —"

"All well and interesting," I said after listening politely for nearly fifteen minutes, "but we're burning daylight."

I pulled out my pocket watch and gave it a windup. It was just nine o'clock in the morning.

"That's an awful nice watch," Slim Reynolds said. "Must've cost you a dollar or two."

"Ten dollars," I said. Don's jaw dropped open in surprise.

"My land, how did you ever afford it?"

"I got it from my wife."

Dodge stepped in. "Let's talk business. How about a swap for our wagon team? Even up — two fresh geldings for our road-weary pair?"

"As you say," Slim said, cautiously eyeing our horses, "they did seem a bit tired when you came in last night."

"We're fixing to pull out to head back to

Yankton this afternoon," Dodge said. "It's a long trip, and I'd like some good horses."

Slim was skeptical. "Yankton's a long ride on a wagon."

Don said, "Never been there, but heard tell it's a rough town."

"Not as rough as the rheumatism pounding hobnails in my knees," Dodge said. "So what does that tell you?"

Slim poked his nose into a damp cross-breeze. If the hometown man knew anything, it was the local weather. "Could be fixing up a blow at that."

I said, "If you don't mind, we'd like to be on the road shortly after noon?"

"If I might ask," Slim said, suddenly all cautious-like, "what's your business in Le Mars?"

Ted Roberts said, "Just passing through."

"Looking for a bite of lunch," Biff said.

Dodge smiled. "Puttin' the clamps to a murderous desperado who's loose in your God-fearin' community before he robs you blind."

Slim Reynolds blinked rapidly while the train of conversation switched tracks. Once his engine was up to steam, Slim said, "Ah, yah. Of course. Okay, sure. Tell us about this . . . ah, renegade you're after."

Dodge filled him in on Albert's history,

and each of us added what we could. When Slim was satisfied with our origin, he said. "Have you notified the law constabulary?"

"What's he talking about?" Ted said.

"We'd prefer to keep your local marshal out of our business," Dodge said.

A filth-encrusted cowpoke straddling an ancient mule trundled past on the street, and Dodge pulled us all in closer to the livery door under its wide striped awning. "No sense folks getting too nosy," he said. "I'd like to ask a favor, if I might."

The brothers communicated with a look, then Slim said, "Whatever we can do to help."

Dodge introduced Biff Barlow to Slim and Don. "Biff is the one man among us who Kid Wade won't recognize. Our plan is to send him out to the Mansfield farm where we've heard the Kid is hiding out. Wondered if you could give us directions?"

"Mansfield's is a nice little place," Don said. "It's right on the crick, sort of built up on an embankment, and they have a big fence built around the yard. Oh, but don't fret," he added, "the gate is always open."

"I'm going to pretend to be a horse scalper," Biff said. "I'll get to looking around and see if Wade is home. If he is, I'll see if he's peddling any stolen ponies."

"I'll be covering him from a distance with this," I said, holding up a pocket spy scope.

"And maybe that?" Slim said, pointing at Dodge's Springfield in its boot on the wagon.

"Maybe that, too," I said, just to get along. Unless the Kid pulled trigger, I didn't plan on pitching any lead.

"Once Biff has a horse picked out, he's gonna pretend to not have enough cash to close the deal."

"That's where you all come in," Biff told the Reynolds brothers. "I'll suggest we visit the bank here in town, then close the deal over a drink at the saloon. I'll bring Kid into the livery to park our horses against the wind."

"Once inside," I told Slim, "you shut the doors of your barn so Kid can't get out. The four of us will draw down on him right then and there."

Gifted with an exciting role in our play, the Reynolds brothers floated a full six inches above the boards and their blinky eyes surely spelled out the Morse code for excitement.

High adventure had come to the town of Lucy, Elizabeth, Mary, Anna, et al., and they were thick in the mix.

They might even become famous.

236

■ ■ ■ ■

Crossing a stubble cornfield under a bright blue sky, I gave Biff a wide berth and approached Mansfield farm from the south while he walked in the front gate with the Reynolds brothers' spare horse. Sneaky as St. Pete, I moved along the creek bank and up a long gradient that rose to a prominent point where I could look down on the farm with my prairie telescope.

Like a pirate from Robert Louis Stevenson's book, I scrunched down my left eye and put the other to the back of my clear, glass lens.

Biff stood inside a red painted fence of tight vertical slats, bolstered by horizontal planks top and bottom, held in place every few feet by deep-rooted cedar posts. The kind of fence you could hide behind. But like Slim promised, the gate stood wide open.

Biff led his pony to the edge of some yellow straw grass and hallooed the two-story frame house.

From my spot on the frosted summit I saw chuffing thick plumes of smoke rise from the tall brick chimney. And wisps of cotton white.

Biff came to a standstill near a round dug well with a round rock foundation, rope, bucket, and crank. From where I crouched on the hill, I couldn't see the front door.

Biff hollered again, and I'm sure they heard him as far back as Long Pine. "Hello?!"

I put a hand to Dodge's Springfield. Slim Reynolds had expected me to take it. Now, as a rough answer came in return to Biff's query, I was glad to have it in hand.

"Who the hell are you?" the voice said.

"A friend. Looking for a drink. You mind if I use your well?"

I heard the voice come back, saw Biff say something again, then watched as a bearded figure entered my view.

I'd never seen the man before, but within three heartbeats, Albert Wade joined him, minus his hat and coat, wearing only boots, pants, and a checkered shirt.

Biff offered the bearded man his hand, then got a drink from the well. When he turned back, Albert said something, Biff faked a laugh, then the beard spoke. Before long, they were chatting away like magpies.

I eased my grip on the rifle, and dropped down to one knee, satisfied with Biff's performance. Now, if only Albert would take the bait and come to town.

My stomach rumbled, despite the breakfast of four fried eggs, bacon, toast, and coffee we'd enjoyed by way of Mrs. Newton at the Le Mars hotel. One thing I always liked about traveling with C.C. Dodge, we ate well. During the course of our trip, the four of us had stayed at three hotels and dined at a half-dozen cafés and saloons along the road. The fat little kitty we had when we left Paddock was sorely depleted, but Ted said he had a plan for raking in some money on the road home. I shuddered to imagine what he had in mind, and so far he wasn't talking.

The next peek through my glass rewarded me with the vision of Biff taking inventory on a gray Oregon horse, branded O-4, around 700 pounds. She wore a gorgeous six-string Southwestern saddle with fine-tooled leather and doghouse stirrups.

I halfway expected to see Shady Jane, and felt a weight lift off my shoulders when I didn't.

"What'cha doing, mister?"

This was the second time in a short while I'd been surprised from behind, and the first time landed me in a case of sore ribs, a loose tooth, and about three-dozen scratches and cuts. I didn't want a repeat performance of my wrestling match with Albert, but more, I

239

didn't want to draw any attention to myself, and on top of it all, I didn't want to take a bullet to the brain pan. So I panicked and performed a kind of awkward shoulder roll that left me face up to my attacker, off balance, and with empty hands.

"Don't be scared."

The boy wasn't more than seven years old, with an untamed mop of red hair, a yarn cap, mittens, and a striped flannel coat that smelled of fried chicken. He wore tall, pointed toe boots and snuffed through his nose with every other word.

"How'd you get the drop on me, amigo?"

The rifle was cockeyed on the ground between us, and I was quick to sit up and grab it.

"My name's not Meego. It's Seth."

"I'm pleased to meet you."

"What are you doing?"

"I'm . . . uh." Seth's curious blue eyes expected an answer. I answered with the innocent truth. "I'm just taking a rest before traveling on."

"You can come down and rest in my house." His face beamed with pride. "We've got a new, warm cookstove."

Another volley of smoke crested the hill. "So I see. That's mighty nice during the winter."

"Daddy and his friend Albert put it to-gether yesterday."

"Your daddy has a friend named Albert? That's funny, I have a friend named Albert."

"Maybe it's the same Albert?"

I shook my head. "No, I don't think so."

"Daddy met Albert in jail."

Before I could answer, Seth bent over and picked up my spyglass. "This is a special treasure."

"It surely is," I said, watching him put it up to his eye. He moved his head in every direction, flashing the scope left and right, up and down.

"You can see a million miles away with it."

"Almost," I said.

"You watching for stars?"

"It's a little too bright during the day for stars," I said.

"Birds, maybe?"

"You know what, Seth? You're exactly right. I'm watching for birds."

I glanced over my shoulder and almost lost my breakfast. The yard in front of the Mansfield house was empty.

Chapter Twenty-One

I scanned the landscape with my spyglass, passing over the fleeting forms of Biff and Albert twice before getting the cornfield in focus. The two were riding side by side at an all-out gallop — Biff on the Oregon horse, Albert on the livery pony.

"Lemme see, mister."

I turned back to Seth and squatted down to his level. "Tell you what, buddy. Let's you and me make a trade — you know, the way the Indians do?"

"I like Indians."

"Here's the swap. You take my spyglass —"

"Hooray!"

I shushed him fast, lowering my own voice to a whisper with hopes he'd follow my lead. "You take my spyglass, and in return, you promise not to tell your dad where you got it or anything about me for the next day or so."

"Until tomorrow?"

"Wait until the day after tomorrow."

"And then I can keep the looking glass?"

"Yes." I slid the tubes together and placed the glass in his mittened hand. He spit in his other hand, and we shook on it.

Then, I lit a shuck under my pants for Ed, who I'd left to graze under a pair of mulberry trees near the foot of the hill.

If Biff and Albert were on their way back to Le Mars, I needed to shake a leg. Especially if Biff was on the big gray in a flat-out gallop.

I lost sight of them while turning around, and at the edge of the cornfield, I came up against a dilemma.

The hayfield ahead showed no signs of life. No badger holes, no mole stumps, no tracks of any kind. If Biff and Albert had gone this direction, they'd left no sign. Which meant this was the direction I should take back into town. Even in the friendliest transaction, Albert was on guard. Looking over his shoulder, he'd recognize Ed right off.

The alternative was worse. If Albert suspected Biff of trickery, he might stop and question him. Maybe fill him with lead right there, or lead him into a trap. Taking the hayfield trail back to Le Mars meant Biff would be alone.

It was a risk I wouldn't take. I came to Iowa because I couldn't abandon Albert. Neither was I going to abandon Biff.

I promised myself to stick with my friends and enemies both until this blasted thing was done. Instead of the hayfield, I pushed Ed along a row of sticktights and thistles until we found a path clearly trod by a pair of horses before us.

I picked up the trail and followed it into town.

Rounding the blacksmith shop onto Main Street afoot with Ed, I located Biff at the Oregon gray's flank not twenty feet in front of the open livery — talking with Albert. The livery horse was beside a hitching post near the bank, and the two men were dickering.

There was little doubt "Sam Gordon" would make his final appeal now that Biff had experienced the wonders of the horse and her luxurious saddle in motion.

I left Ed in front of a saloon water trough and took to the boardwalk, keeping my back to the street as I moved along, watching Biff and Al in the reflection of the shop windows. Once I got close enough to hear, I listened in on their negotiation.

"— meaning to keep her," Albert said, "but times being what they are, I need the money for my family. She's less than two years old. I raised her from a colt."

"You're a good man, Mr. Gordon."

"Like I said before, you call me Sam." Then: "Anyway, I just can't see fit to give her away for nothing."

Biff said he understood, and wasn't she a fine horse, and how if he had a horse like her, he could never part with her for less than $150. "So I'm offering you $152 for the mare and the saddle both."

One thing about Biff was that he never lost the patter from the days when he and his brother ran around tricking people. Or the knack of telling a lie. Such a sly talent might seem common on first thought, but it's a skill relatively few men possess.

Standing on the boardwalk of Le Mars, Iowa, I listened to two masters of the craft.

"My final offer is $152," Biff said. "Cash money. You've already got the $10 I gave you back at the farm."

Albert was speechless at the insult. "It's an insult," he said. "Especially with the saddle. Do you know I had that handmade a year or so back while visiting Arizona? My price of $200 is rock bottom."

"I'll go $153."

"I've sold ten-year-old mules with nothing but a blanket for more."

"What do you think she's worth, Mr. Gordon?"

"Like I said, I wouldn't sell her for less than $200."

"Tell you what," Biff said, "I'll give you $160, plus I'll toss in $3 in oats from the livery barn for the trade pony."

Why not? Now that we had the horse in hand, it was ours to take back as evidence.

Al pretended to think about Biff's offer. Finally, he stuck out his hand. "Done deal."

"Aw, I sure do appreciate it, Mr. Gordon, I sure do."

Then Albert plucked the gray's reins from Biff's grip. "How about I'll keep your new purchase safe until you secure the cash from your account. You go to the bank. I'll meet you over at the saloon."

"Hold on now, Mr. Gordon." Biff was quick on the uptake. "You're not trying to back out on me?"

"Just watching my back."

"Sounds like what I'll be doing as you run off with my down payment?"

Albert said, "How do I know you'll show up at the saloon?"

Biff clapped his hands. "We'll strike a balance. You ever heard of an escrow account?

We'll let the livery man hold both horses while I go to the bank, and you go to the saloon."

Albert looked around the street, and I pulled down the brim of my hat.

"I think it suits me okay," he said. Then he followed Biff into the livery barn.

Three steps behind, I slipped in just before Slim rolled the door shut.

Shadow enveloped the open center space of the barn with its five stalls on each side. Albert spun around as hard beams of sunlight shone through the tin-covered walls, pinning him in dusty lattice work. "What goes on here?"

Biff had his Peacemaker pointed straight at Albert's forehead. "You're caught, Kid."

"You filthy, rotten —"

"Save it, Albert." I came around from behind Biff with Dodge's Springfield rifle ready to fire.

The confusion and betrayal on Albert's face nearly tore me in two. "Not you, August John?"

Dodge and Ted Roberts pushed open the gates of opposite horse pens and moved in behind.

"We've come to take you home, boy."

Albert pivoted — one way, then another. He thrust a hand toward his chest.

"Hands up," Biff said, the muzzle of his gun less than an inch from Albert's ear.

Albert tossed his arms high, and Dodge secured a gun from inside the Kid's coat. "Looky here. A British Bulldog." He dropped it into his own coat pocket. "Not what I would've expected from such a highly celebrated lawbreaker."

"On your knees, Kid." Ted lunged forward, cracking the butt of his scattergun against Albert's calves, folding his legs in half. His knees cracked like plaster slamming into the packed sod floor.

"Not so rough," I said.

Ted smirked. "What're you, his mother?"

"Tie him up," Dodge said, all but ignoring Albert as he strode around him toward Biff and me. He put a hand on my shoulder in passing, then nodded for Slim to slide back the door.

The Reynolds brothers opened the barn, and the forenoon light came in brash and shining.

Dodge gave Slim a gold dollar — one of our last — and said, "Send this message to Sheriff Barnabus Welton in O'Neill: We have the Kid. Put a man on a horse and communicate with our wives. No one hurt. C.C. Dodge, Capt. Chelsea Regulators."

Slim scurried off to deliver the good news.

Grounded in the sights of the rifle and Biff's six-shooter, Kid Wade chewed the inside of his mouth while Ted jerked his arms back and wrapped a rope around his wrists. Enraged, his stomach moving in and out with rapid, hot breath, Albert was like a trapped animal — scared and snarling.

I lowered the rifle. "Nobody's gonna hurt you."

Ted put his face close to Albert's cheek. "We'll carve that on your tombstone."

Albert spit in his eye, got clocked on the temple with the shotgun for his trouble, and fell over sideways.

Ted slapped at his brow, stung and embarrassed, "I should kill you now and save the good folks of Nebraska the cost of a trial."

From where he stood talking with the Reynolds brothers, Dodge spoke around the match he chewed, "Play nice, Ted."

"Just get him into the wagon," Biff said.

"You done a hell of a job acting your part," Albert told him. "You had me fooled, and that ain't easy to do."

"He's had plenty of practice fooling people," Ted said. "Takes a crook to catch a crook."

Biff outweighed Ted nearly two to one and bellied up close to him. "You should be careful the way you talk about your friends."

Ted snickered. "Another epithet I'll probably see carved in limestone."

Albert said, "What's your name, anyway? Your real name?"

"This is Biff Barlow," I said.

"Biff, I'd like you to have that saddle. You ask the owner of that Oregon gray when you see him; it's not his. Honest to gosh, it's my own saddle — and you did such a fine job of snookering me, I want you to have it to remember me by."

It was just the kind of magnanimous gesture the Kid was known for, and Biff couldn't hide his surprise. "Who does the Oregon gray belong to?"

Albert shrugged. "I can't say I remember now."

I asked Biff: "Were there any other stolen horses at the farm?"

"Didn't see any. No sign of Shady Jane, that's for sure."

Slim Reynolds said, "Word from out west is there's a storm blowing in. If you boys are gonna beat it across the Missouri, you better get a move on."

I ignored the show and pulled out my watch. "Let's go, boys. We're running out of time."

Worried about the weather, we pounded

back over the hills, west to the Missouri River, Dodge pushing the new team of Le Mars horses as hard as he dared with Ted and Albert battered by the road, bouncing along in the wagon box.

On the way into Iowa we ate well and slept better and took the time to have fun, whether teasing Ted about his bone collection or telling smutty jokes since there weren't any gals around.

The way home was all business.

Dodge figured if we could make it to Yankton, we could wait for the storm to pass before advancing on to the Niobrara valley.

Biff and I rode behind on our horses, occasionally sharing a smoke, but mostly hammering out the miles.

It was too dark to get careless with navigation. We were rolling too fast to converse. We rode more than twenty hours straight through, and I do believe I still have a stitch in my side that flares up now and then because of it. My butt felt like ground sausage without the casing. My arms ached, my fingers ached, and no amount of alcohol could slow down the pulse of my nerves. So I didn't drink any when Dodge offered.

When it was dark, Albert slept. During the day, as the temperature dropped and the wind picked up, he hooted and hollered.

"You gonna take me to your uncle's house, Ted? Lord knows, I've enjoyed many a fine meal with Henry Richardson."

Or, "How about we go door to door in Holt County and inspect every brand on every horse available? You boys might lose some more sleep."

It was something we all got used to during the next several days, Albert spreading around enough blame to hang all of Brown County for schemers and connivers, horse thieves and killers.

Some of what he said was true.

CHAPTER TWENTY-TWO

February 5, 1884

The streets of Long Pine were a winter wonderland blanketed with snow, a holy oasis of family, hearth, and cookstove. Cherry pies and prairie hens. Or, in the Barker Room of the hotel, a kind of open dance hall used for dinners and family reunions, a bizarre circus of upside-down values and unholy debauchery. Take your pick.

There were at least fifty hot, sweaty men, women, and children stuffed into the long, rectangular hot box, all of them having paid fifty cents a head to see the notorious outlaw, Kid Wade, and marvel at his antics.

Wrists and ankles secured in irons, Albert sat on a veritable throne, a chair made of walnut carved full of goofy dog heads and cat paws, and a seat of blue velvet. Perched atop of a steamer trunk perpendicular to five rows of folding tables and chairs, he looked down on the evening diners from under his felt hat.

The girls of Long Pine baked pie with canned peaches and served baked ham and scalloped potatoes with cheese burnt dark brown across the top in a crust. I picked up a dinner roll from the serving table in the hotel dining room, took a bite, chewed, thought about putting it back.

"Hey, August John! Toss that biscuit in the air, and I'll perforate it right through the middle with my trusty six-shooter. That is . . . if I had one!"

Kid Wade could do it too. He cackled away madly.

I decided I wasn't hungry, so I stuffed the bread in my pants pockets and dropped out of the serving line, wondering just how many people the noisy, cramped room could hold before it burst. Thirty, forty . . . more?

"Come one, come all," Albert shouted. "Ain't that how you call a circus?"

Henry Richardson leaned in and slapped him with his bandanna.

Finding a corner of unoccupied floor space behind the crowd and as far away from Albert as I could get, I pulled in a chair and sat down. Put my aching head in my hands.

The last few weeks had become a blur.

I was exhausted. Biff, Ted, and Dodge

weren't much better. We boys who'd seen the entire road through from Le Mars were spent. We needed the traveling show to end — what Albert rightly called a circus.

A boy with his mouth full of ham and gravy called out, "When are you gonna show us some rope tricks, Kid?"

His buddy said, "I wanna see you shoot!"

Albert's face shined like the sun. He'd gotten plenty of rest.

Henry Richardson told the boys to wait until after the meal. "Then you'll see some real action."

Albert smoked an expensive black cigar and wore his hat at a rakish angle. A dozen people stood an arm's-length away, marveling at his presence while Ted Roberts stood close, shotgun in hand.

"Here's the celebrated bad man of a thousand vanished horses," Ted said. "Expert with revolver and rope, professor of sin and depravity, Kid Wade will soon perform feats reserved only for those with a proficiency in dark deeds."

Which was stupid, because I could out-rope Albert, and even Ted was as good with a pistol. The whole line of talk was a dirty sham to prey on the gullible townsfolk, most of who responded to the pitch like Jesus was coming down on a cloud.

I was sick of dealing with the gleefully curious, the morbidly fascinated, the wealthy, privileged thrill seekers.

We'd been fending the gawkers off since Yankton and our first night at the Commercial Hotel. Kid Wade's fame preceded him because we were immediately called on by cops and lawyers and reporters from the press. Three of Albert's old gal friends showed up, and Doctor Livingston from Niobrara checked to make sure we hadn't broken his arms or shot him or anything.

We didn't have any money, and Ted Roberts decided to put Albert on display to generate some cash. He made arrangements with the Turner Room, a prestigious community center, but a local church minister shut us down.

Typical. But God bless the man, anyway.

The longer we stayed in those Dakota back rooms, the stranger things got. The snow flew, the money flowed, and I never saw Ted Roberts work harder at anything else in his life. He figured we had an opportunity here — why not exploit it?

The authorities wanted Albert to stay in Yankton and answer for a Dakota wagon he stole once, and Dodge wanted to go pick up the Kid's brother-in-law in a nearby town. I was glad when we left the whole country to get closer to home.

I didn't find out how we paid for the nights in Yankton until three years later when Dodge told me he borrowed money from Slim Reynolds in Le Mars.

From Yankton it was on to Redbird, where we put the Kid into Cap Burnham and Richardson's hands. They asked him some questions and roughed him up a little at Back Berry's Paddock cow pen.

"You're as big a horse thief as I am," Albert told Henry Richardson, echoing what John Wade had said to me — though he never knew it.

Outraged at the public accusation, Henry pulled a revolver and was two shakes from ending the whole affair when I stepped in front of the gun.

It's the reason I came along in the first place. I wanted justice for all of Albert's victims, but I wanted justice for Albert, too.

After that, we moved on, through an endless parade of way stations and regulator homes, the wives showing great hospitality, the men getting their swipes in.

They were all so obsessed, had lived so long for this moment of victory. It seemed like scrawny, unrepentant Albert Wade was something of a letdown for them.

Finally, we ended up in Long Pine, with

nobody sure how to run the kind of legal proceedings that would satisfy everybody. Nobody yet had the nerve to go against us and throw a necktie party.

But without any official county guidelines, we were a cluster of squabbling brats.

"I see you boys made the newspaper." I turned to accept the gracious hand of Lester Linsenbardt, an old corn-shucker from Carns. He held up a copy of the *Holt County Banner,* and I read the front page story. Somebody had shared the ordeal at Berry's pen involving Richardson, and the paper aimed to shape public opinion:

It is reported here that at the examination at Berry's the Kid told Henry Richardson, a member of the Brown County company, that he was as big a horse thief as him (the Kid). Whereupon Richardson wanted to shoot him while he was in shackles but was prevented from doing so. Now, we have no sympathy for Kid Wade, neither have we any respect or sympathy for a man who will try to shoot another when he is powerless to defend himself. We believe the majority of the vigilanters to be honorable, respectable men, but in our humble opinion they should purge their ranks of such characters as Richardson if they

258

expect to retain the confidence of the people.

I handed the paper back to Lester. "Don't believe anything you hear," I said, "and only half of what you read."

"Knowing Henry, I guess I believe he did just what they say he did." I watched him rejoin the crowd.

Across the Barker Room, Albert took the cigar out of his mouth and blew a smoke ring. Then he blew a smoke ring through the center of the first.

I thought two of the ladies in attendance would faint.

Biff Barlow carried his plate over and stood beside me. Watching Ted deliver his message I said, "Remind you of anybody?"

"Shut up," he said — but good-natured. He knew I was talking about him and his brother, and he didn't mind being put through the fire a bit. "I was more convincing than Ted will ever be." He turned to look at me, his rosy cheeks aglow. We sat near the stove, and just over my shoulder, a row of expensive glass windows put the ongoing winter bluster on exhibit. There must've been three inches of fresh snow on the ground, but it was falling even, without a wind.

A pretty picture if it would have had a frame.

Now that we had Albert in custody, my entire life felt that way. Everything up for show.

I drank coffee in honor of Trudy, and Biff sipped his beer. We watched Ted hand out hand-printed flyers to old women and children.

Biff said, "Albert has committed serious crimes — far more than any fool prank I ever pulled. Yet, here he is, treated like a heroic figure."

I watched the two young boys from before, dressed in flannel shirts, dark pants, and straw hats run around in a circle while their ma stood enraptured by Ted's voice. The boys kept their thumbs and index fingers cocked and smoking. "Bang, bang, bang!"

"Now, for those of you interested in the particulars of how this ruffian was brought to justice by yours truly and my band of regulators, I'll be offering the full, un-adorned story in fifteen minutes."

"I want to hear, Mommy! I want to hear!" One of the little kids aimed his finger at Albert. "Bang, bang!" he cried, and Albert clutched his chest, pretending to be shot. At the last minute, he aimed back with his finger and said, "Pow!" but the kid didn't play along.

"Those urchins there don't need Kid's bad example," Biff said.

I shrugged. "There's more than one kind of bad example."

"Gotta be hell for Albert."

"You know what I think, Biff? I think Albert is having a dandy of a time."

"I'd hate getting marched out and put on a stage."

"Truth is, it's all Albert's ever lived for."

Together, we watched C.C. Dodge enter from a far entrance and join Ted next to Albert. He whispered something in his ear, turned, and nodded at us — then left the room. As always, he didn't so much as look in Albert's direction.

Ted Roberts exhorted his grateful congregation to come back after the meal for his sermon. When he joined us in the corner, he carried a roll of money as big around as his arm, and just as green.

On the other side of the room, Albert relaxed in his chair, relishing the expensive cigar, folding his hands over his stomach. He closed his eyes in a moment of obvious bliss.

"What's next?" I said. "Where do we go from here?"

"I guess it's up to Burnham," Ted said.

"Me? I could take this show all over the country."

"We can't keep Albert locked up forever," I said.

"Why not?"

I excused myself and wandered through the crowd, noting all the big names rubbing shoulders with each other. The founders of Brown County, some fellows from Holt and Knox. Virgil Manke held court at a table all his own, and I noticed his wife carried her own personal teapot. It was easier to say who wasn't there that night than who was.

Ben Frymire wasn't there. Neither was Trudy.

I walked past the throne and was hailed.

Albert said, "You watch out for that one, August John."

"Who?" I followed his eyes. "Ted Roberts?"

"Crazy as a closet full of bats."

"He's still full of piss and vinegar."

"He's full of himself most of all. One day somebody'll drain his jug dry."

"Maybe. But it won't be you. And it won't be me."

"Ted can't tie a knot worth a durn." Albert's face loved to smile, and he showed me his teeth while pulling his arms as far apart as the chain between his wrist irons would allow. "Guess that's why I'm in these."

"You want me to get you anything? Cup of coffee?"

He said no, and so we talked awhile.

He mentioned the weather ("It always snows when I go to Dakota — I should've told you up front.") and his opinion of C. C. Dodge ("A good driver. Handled his wagon team like a dream.").

For my part, I enjoyed telling Albert about how, on the way to Le Mars, we had teased Ted with the story of the bone collector. "He ended up with a fifty pound sack of prairie bones to barter."

"He had his bones on the way over. You've got your prairie bones on the way back." His laugh was full of phlegm. "Guess I don't weigh in too heavy."

"You callin' yourself a sack of prairie bones?"

"Ain't that what any of us are — skull and bones? Walking around, talking, pitching sheep-dip for a while, then chucked out to the clay." He rolled his shoulders and tried to stretch his legs. His ankles were bound in shackles. "Right about now, I wouldn't mind two or three million years of sleep."

"One day the circus will be over. You'll do some time in jail. You'll be released. Just like before. Just like Doc Middleton."

"Now who's boneheaded?"

"What's that supposed to mean?"

"You heard Ted back in the Le Mars stable. None of these boys will rest until they can carve up my tombstone."

"You're going to have a fair trial."

"God, I hope not."

"You should've turned yourself in to me at Plum Creek."

"Let's say I was protecting you. Like you're trying to do for me now."

"It didn't make any difference," I said.

He smiled and closed his eyes as the crowd started to gather around us. "That's exactly what I've been trying to tell you. Nothing ever does."

We walked outside in the snow, Cap Burnham, Virgil Manke, and me, the two older men smoking cigars, me with my hands shoved deep in my pants pockets. Within the hotel, the crowd cheered to hear Ted Roberts's exploits, booing and hissing whenever Albert raised his voice. They were all having a grand time.

Burnham had a nice Stetson like the one Frymire wore. Manke left his head exposed, his thick white hair and mustache giving his expression an extra cold demeanor. Dressed in heavy coats, they kept a multitude of guns hidden away in their pockets. Everybody acted like Albert was gonna jump up and mow down the entire state.

I was dressed in a sweater with no hat. The wind was cold on my ears.

Burnham said, "Come morning, I'm driving Albert to Morris's Bridge where I'll turn him over to the Holt County sheriff."

Manke stopped in his tracks. "You're not."

"Yes, by God, I am," Cap said, his voice rising by just the smallest degree. "We can't keep hauling him around the country. It's not right or respectable. We've got to show some kind of leadership."

Manke said, "Put him through a morning trial right here in Long Pine — fair and square. We'll hang him tomorrow night."

"There's nothing fair about what you said. Do you even hear yourself, Virgil?"

"We all know he's guilty."

"The new sheriff in O'Neill is Ed Hershiser —"

"And Hershiser has no jurisdiction in Brown County."

"He's got just as much power as you or I do," Cap said. "Add to that, he's got an official warrant for the arrest of Kid Wade. If he asks, I'm obligated to comply." Cap held out a telegram. "This came over the wire today. Hershiser is asking."

Manke couldn't hide the scorn in his voice. "A warrant means somebody swore a complaint within a given time frame." He pointed at the telegram with his chin. "He's bluffing you. There's no legal warrant."

"Yes, there is," I said. "Because I'm the one who swore the complaint."

I had never been able to pull the wool over Cap's eyes, and I never did again. But that day on the street in Long Pine, he was as shocked as Virgil Manke. "You, Gus?"

Manke cursed. "I'd like to know one good goddamn reason why."

My own frustration boiled out of me, and I put more heat on Manke than I probably should have. "Virgil, you were there at Back Berry's place. You saw Henry Richardson level his gun at Albert. If we keep parading him back and forth like this, somebody's going to kill him. Is that what you want on your conscience?"

"I could pull the trigger myself. I'd sleep just fine, thank you."

Cap said, "It's not the way we agreed to do things last fall."

I said, "Remember the document we all signed? We sat at your table. In your house."

Manke's reply made my skin crawl. "Fellows, that document no longer exists."

266

Cap said, "What's that supposed to mean?"

"You should've taken it to Carns with you, Burnham. As it was, I've had some flooding in my basement. Unfortunately, the rain got into my safe." Manke showed us his open palms and puffed mightily on his cigar. "I'm afraid a good many of my legal documents were ruined. Including the charter for the Niobrara Mutual Protective Association."

Cap said, "Willfully destroying a legal contract is —"

"Nothing willful about it. Like I said . . . it was an accident." He pulled the cigar from his mouth. "Call it an act of God."

"Either way," I said, "Ed Hershiser will be at Morris's Bridge tomorrow."

"The question," Manke said, "is whether Kid Wade will be at that bridge." He slapped his hands together and rubbed the arms of his coat. "I dare say, it is getting chilly out here, isn't it boys?"

At Martin's Long Pine hotel, and against his ongoing complaints, we kept Albert chained overnight. Biff added extra restraints, clamping Albert's bound arms to the headboard of his bed. Cap agreed to stand guard outside while Biff and I stayed in the room, sleeping in shifts.

267

Once everybody settled in, Albert snored like a newborn baby, well-fed and content. Lucky him.

CHAPTER TWENTY-THREE

February 6, 1884

In the foggy, cold morning, Ted Roberts ate breakfast with me before riding home to Virgil Manke's place. Runny cold eggs, but the bacon was nice and crisp. I ate four slices on toast with butter and salt. With Cap, Biff, and me headed to Morris's Bridge with Albert, the other vigs were going home. Ted ate as much as me, maybe more. "I've got a big job proving up on Manke's barn," he said, just because he knew I was working on the barn at Pleasant Valley.

C.C. Dodge had a long ride back to Paddock, and I saw him off with a wave before sitting down to the morning table.

Ted was halfway through his second plate of grub, napkin tucked into the front of his shirt. He pushed up his glasses. "Did you know they wanted to name this place Silver Springs, after the freshwater springs on

Manke's farm? Of course they called it Long Pine because of the trees sprouting up every which way from the canyon."

"I didn't know that." But of course, everybody knew it. I just wanted to keep the peace and get away as quick as I could. I was already a little bit late.

Ted shoveled in another mouthful. "I got to tell you, Gus. It's a joy working out there for Virgil. Even in the cold weather months."

"A man's lucky to find good work."

"You ought to come down during timber season. We can always use an extra set of muscles harvesting timber."

"I might just do that."

Ted put his napkin to his pockmarked face. I noticed he hadn't shaved for a few days, and his white-headed carbuncles left bald spots in his beard. Of course, with so many distractions, I myself hadn't been as religious with a razor as I should've. Ted stroked his whiskered chin. "Once Holt County stretches Albert's neck, I suspect the rest of his desperadoes will be easy enough to round up."

"I suspect so," I said, feeling gloomy at the thought.

"Clip off the head, the roots whither."

I guess he was right about that. I finished eating what I could, then pushed myself away from the table.

"Truth is," Ted said, "I wish I had Albert on hand for another few weeks. We could travel around the country, put on a trick rope show like we did last night. We'd make a fortune."

"I've already got a fortune," I said, thinking about Trudy.

"You've got it good enough," he conceded. "But listen, if some of us old-time Pony Boys got it into our heads, we could put on a show like that by ourselves. Some riding and roping? Some trick shooting? You think about it." He had it all worked out how we'd be multimillionaires before we were thirty.

"Like I said, I've got plenty of things to tend to back home. Time I started getting to it."

I tossed my napkin to my plate and turned my back on him.

Then I plodded to the livery stable with my bottom lip poked out. Ted's words had me brooding. He seemed to think everything we'd been doing was a game. He for sure imagined it as a contest. When I got to the livery stable, I met Henry Richardson and Virgil Manke at the door. "Morning, boys."

Manke nodded. Richardson said, "It's about time. Where you been, Gus?"

"Listening to your nephew's plans for a

show bill."

"Ted's full of ideas. You have to ignore him."

Which is what I did best, but I didn't say so. We walked inside without another word. Biff and Cap Burnham sat on the bench seat of a buckboard wagon with Albert squeezed in between them, trussed up and ready to go.

"I don't appreciate being kept waiting," Cap said.

Manke said, "Gus forgot to wind his watch."

Albert looked around the inside of the barn. "Hard to believe this is goodbye to Long Pine. Yes, sir. Had a lot of good times here, didn't we, Gus?"

"Hard to recall them all, Albert." I had already been to the stable that morning before breakfast to saddle Ed up for the trip. Now that everybody was ready to go, I climbed onto his back.

"Tell you what, Gus," said Albert. "During the next few hours, whatever happens, you try to remember for me. Remember all the good times. Will you do that for me, Gus?"

"I've always been your friend, Al. You were just too bullheaded to see it."

Then the Kid turned his attention to Cap.

I hadn't seen him so chatty since before he went to prison. "I appreciate your turning me over to Hershiser," he said. "This way I'm sure to be killed quick and efficient. All this to and fro around the place was wearing me out."

Manke said, "How about you do us all a favor now, and shut the hell up?" He asked Cap, "What's your route?"

Cap said, "Up the canyon road, then hand off the prisoner to Hershiser. From there we'll roll cross-country to the east. I'll wire you when we get to O'Neill."

"If you get to O'Neill," Henry Richardson said.

"I suspect I've jostled a horse and wagon through the snow before. Today's weather ain't so different."

"Wasn't necessarily talking about the weather."

"I understand that, Henry," Cap said, flicking the reins. "But we'll let you know anyway."

So our adventure began, and it was a wandering, sort of aimless trek at first, because no matter what Cap assumed, it really was different weather, the most fierce wind and sleet I'd ever passed through. I kept my face turned down into my collar, and my hat was pulled down tight. There were times when the wagon blurred out beside me, and only water-filled slushy green wheel ruts gave her away.

After handing over the prisoner at Morris's Bridge, we'd proceed to O'Neill with the sheriff by way of the Holt County road. It had to be all official and legal, and the way we said things was important, but all that "handing over" meant was that we'd follow Hershiser's horse, him leading the way to the Holt County seat. Biff and I planned to see Albert safely secured, then spend the night in O'Neill. We'd ride back to the Keya Paha the next day, unless the snow got too deep or the temperature dropped. We didn't really know what the future had in store.

We'd made it this far, we could make it a little longer.

Sloppy and clinging to all of us, the tepid rude snow was a dirty gray phlegm, coughed from the clouds in unpredictable fits, stinging my cheeks and ears, hanging from our whiskers and eyelashes. Biff was a grumpy marshmallow lump, keeping the port side of the wagon weighed down in the mire, and Cap held the gritty, wet reins, all his attention focused on the horses.

Between the two men, Albert sang songs of bawdy girls and rowdy boys, apparently having the time of his life. Sometimes when I couldn't see the wagon for sheep-dip, I'd hear his lungs burst forth, as in days of old, and it didn't surprise me.

I supposed "Slippery Jack" might have had a way out I didn't perceive, but mostly it was Albert being Albert — long past caring what happened to him. At this point in his life he'd accomplished all he'd ever wanted to do. The newspapers called him a *Captain* — just like Burnham or how they sometimes referred to Dodge or Tarbell. Without ever garnering government sanction for a single act, Albert had led men into battle, conquered enemies, achieved objectives, and been rewarded with fame — fortune too, and didn't Ted think that's what it was all about?

But most times, Kid Wade didn't have two nickels to his name. His fortune was different, and not like the one I imagined in Pleasant Valley.

Albert's fortune was comprised of true freedom. That kind of freedom came with its own price.

Through a lifetime of effort and conniving that rivaled the railroad barons and steel magnates, Albert acquired true autonomy, but he had climbed as far as he could go. As sure as Alexander, Caesar, or Carnegie, he ruled over an empire of property and men. He was feared by some and revered by others. Looking down his ladder at how far he'd come, he might have decided there was no place else to go. Maybe his active philosophy had come to an inevitable fruition, and his genius was in the existential realization of it all.

Or maybe he was just a creepy little shit who was crazy in the head.

Either way, plodding along, listening to him warble all the old songs like a field sparrow, I realized it was the last time in my life I'd likely ever ride with him.

I figured out later that life is funny that way. Sometimes you know it's the last time you'll see somebody you've always known, or the last time you'll visit the house where you grew up. Other times, you never quite know what happened to so-and-so, or such-and-such a place — people and things snatched away from you by rash, darting circumstance.

Or worn away by time.

Sometimes, you just drift along seeing less and less of people, stopping by fewer times to homes or gathering places. Years go by and you try to imagine what happened. Somebody tells you a story or drops a name and it fires something in your head that makes you curious.

What happened?

When we met Ed Hershiser — a likable burly gent with a Boss of the Plains atop his head to rival Frymire's hat — I knew I'd always remember what happened to Kid Wade and where I was when it happened.

I thought the finale to the play would be later that night in an O'Neill, Nebraska, jail cell.

But the horses were laboring. There was no end to the snow. We were all losing patience.

Hershiser wasn't taking any chances.

We made a hard right-hand turn and took the short road to Bassett.

He decided we should catch a train.

CHAPTER TWENTY-FOUR

Martin's Hotel in Bassett, Nebraska, swarmed with people of all ages and old country languages. Refugees from the blizzard, some needed blankets, and some had extra to share. They shared with folks who had less. The stoves churned out heat by the cord-load as Martin's boys humped wood to leave in a tall stack. The place was filled with the careful joy, the next morning's train promising warm, welcome escape.

When Cap Burnham pulled his wagon in behind Sheriff Ed, we trundled our soggy carcasses into the bar room where I'd seen the church ladies prepare chickens and Ted Roberts had served coffee. Here at the counter, we found out there were no vacant beds in the hotel and got ready to settle in on the saloon floor with a dozen others.

Mrs. Martin was as good-natured about the whole scene as anybody could be, and she assigned us a corner space at the wall farthest away from the door. "You ready to eat a few chicken gizzards this time, Gus?" It was nice to know she remembered me from when I'd been there in the fall.

It was late afternoon, but Hershiser and me set up camp with our backs to the paneling, spreading a few blankets into pallets for sleep.

The five of us played cards and another guest named Roy strummed a Jew's harp to keep us entertained. A pair of middle-aged blond twins stayed near us. One old gal took a real shine to Cap, but he pretended not to notice.

"How about a song, Albert?" I said, but Kid had fallen into a dark mood since our arrival and declined. When supper came, he barely ate a chicken wing, and I nearly broke a promise to myself when I agreed to go in on a bottle of rum with him and Biff. "Just for the three of us."

But Cap wasn't drinking, and neither was the sheriff, and I guess that was good for me because I thought better of it at the last minute. "You go ahead without me, Biff." But he ended up drinking coffee, too.

Had we been drunk, we might've got it in our heads to help Kid Wade escape. Leastways, that's what I might have done.

Which is to say I felt sad and sore about

the entire affair, but sober enough to carry on. I still imagined Albert would get out alive.

The snow let up, and the skies cleared as darkness fell. Most of the room's afternoon occupants decided to move on with their horse and wagons, which surprised me, but the waxing moon was bright, so they could see well enough. You can't keep settlers or sodbusters down long before they need to shake the straw out and get to shucking corn.

That old moon shined through the stained glass over the door, and the eerie orange glow made the room seem to flicker like it was on fire. Our new friend Roy tossed some wood into the heat stove and put away his music-maker. One of the blond twins said a goodnight prayer, and I sat next to Albert while he pretended to sleep.

Sometime around 11 o'clock Albert wanted to go to the privy and I said I'd take him, but the sheriff said, no, he would, so I waited with a gnawing hunch in my gut.

Would Albert make a break for it?

I couldn't imagine him overpowering a husky guy like Hershiser, especially all cuffed and tied, but I'd been tricked once too often by Albert to get too complacent. When the two of them came back in and Al sagged down next to me, my stomach cleared up.

Like I'd shared my worries aloud, he said, "I decided not to make a run for it after all."

"Is that the way you were thinking?"

"Sure, what do you think? Why wouldn't I? Did you think it was somebody else other than ol' Slippery Jack sitting here beside you?"

"I thought maybe you had incentive not to run. Maybe Sheriff Ed would shoot you in your tracks."

"That friendly ol' mutt? I hardly think so."

"So if you weren't afraid of the sheriff, why didn't you run?"

He chewed on it awhile, then said, "Maybe you've got me convinced to look at a new way of life."

"It's a little late now."

"Is it?" He held up his arms so only I could see them. "Is it too late?" The iron shackles slid down, off his arms into his lap.

A jolt shot through my guts, lifting me to my knees. I put my hand on the gun in my holster, whispering hard and fast. "Don't make a move, Albert."

His laugh was soft but full in the back of his throat, and he eased down, back against the wall. "Here ya go." He handed me a silver key. "If you want to lock me up again. I've been practicing all day."

"How'd you get a key?"

"I rode twenty miles squashed between Burnham and Barlow. You think Slippery Jack can't lift a key in such time?"

"You're not playing fair."

"I have never pretended to be anything other than I am." It was one of those things he always said to prove his high moral ground. Like pillaging a neighbor was okay as long as you weren't a hypocrite about it.

"Such bullshit," I said, exasperated but still whispering. "Every time I turn around you're pretending."

"I beg to differ."

"Sam Gordon."

"Okay, but aside from that."

"Singing and dancing and smoking cigars for Ted's shows."

"That wasn't pretending."

"Sure it was. Pretending you weren't scared."

Which shut him up pretty fast, but he came back a few minutes later. "The whole damn valley is cursed, you know. It's been that way since before the Ponca drive and before the Sioux came. Living there, we can't help what we become. That's the curse of the Niobrara, Gus. We're destined for whatever it wants us to be."

"What we become . . . is up to each one of us to decide."

"Wouldn't that be nice."

"You're surrounded by men who decide every day," I said. "Look at Cap Burnham. He's got a property, a good family, a law career. He'll likely end up in the government one day. Or what about Biff Barlow? There's a man who changed his tune since I met him last fall."

Albert's tone was snide and condescending. "Okay. What about Henry Richardson or Ted Roberts, always making threats to stretch somebody's neck? What about Virgil Manke and his barn?"

"Some of the boys act up now and — wait," I said. "What about Virgil Manke and his barn?"

Albert's moonlit smile was grim, his lips like red sealing wax keeping his message to himself.

"What about Virgil Manke?" I said again.

"Is it worth sharing a swig of rum?"

I sat quietly for a minute. He tried again.

"You mentioned rum earlier. You get us a drink, we'll talk."

I turned my head. "All right," I said, "but you tell me first."

He leaned in close.

He told me.

That's when Cap stood up and stepped over the two snoring twins to peer out a front window. When he came back to our corner, he edged across the wooden floor over to my blanket. "Did you hear something?"

"Like what? I didn't hear anything."

"That?" He cocked his head. I strained to identify the sound he had heard. "Like a footstep."

I got up on my haunches. "Yeah, I heard it." We stood up.

The outside door to the saloon broke up with a crash and four men charged in. They carried pistols and a shotgun. They wore heavy long dark coats and black hoods over their heads with holes cut out for eyes. The leader made his demands clear.

"We're here for Kid Wade."

Hershiser was up, palming his revolver. "Drop the guns. Kid Wade is under our protection." Cap stood beside him, and I joined them.

Aiming my pistol, I put a bead on the first masked man's chest. "You heard the sheriff. Drop the guns."

The masked man pulled his trigger and glass shattered just over the heads of the two blond women. "It's you who's gonna hand over the guns."

The shotgun man swung around, pulled the trigger, and three bottles on the counter went up in a massive explosion of shards. "Do it now."

Without further protest, the sheriff tossed his gun into the center of the saloon floor.

Cap followed suit.

Surprised me like I was a newborn pup, but they didn't want the twin blond gals caught in a cross fire.

The man with the shotgun called me by name. "What about it, Gus?"

I stopped breathing. Caught between moments, unsure. Frozen.

Albert stood up, jerked the pistol from my sweaty grip, tossed it down to the floor. "No use innocent people getting hurt," he said.

"We'll be sure to get that carved onto your tombstone," the shotgun man said.

Giving himself away.

Kid Wade stood in the center of the Martin's Hotel saloon, red and orange stained glass coloring his features, mustering up all the sincerity he could manage.

He asked the masked men for a second chance.

"You boys let me go with the sheriff and appeal to the good people of Holt County,

285

and I swear I'll be a better man than I have been."

It's the last thing I ever heard him say.

While the two armed vigilantes threatened us with gunfire, the other two shoved through and grabbed up Albert, one on each arm. They plucked him out of our posse like pulling a noxious weed from a garden, his boots trailing across the wood floor like torn roots.

As soon as they were out the door, we scooped up our guns and rushed the door, while the other guests dropped comments and made up fictions.

"Did you hear his voice? I'm sure one of them is Irish."

"One of them carried an old Remington pistol."

"No, no — it was a Colt, and he was double-fisting a pair of them."

"One of them was a woman, sure as I'm standing here."

At the edge of the broken doorway, I heard a wrangling of horses and a gusty "Hee-yaww!" and a wagon trundled past, tossing up frozen clods of mud and snow, picking up speed. One masked man was on the bench, flailing a whip over a team of four chargers. Two of the vigs held Kid Wade in the box. The one with the shotgun was still on foot.

I bulled past Cap and Sheriff Hershiser, bounding into a sprint up the street, launching myself at the last possible second into a wild attack that brought the masked vig and me into a bone-crunching collision with the road.

I rolled to one side, both arms wrapped around the masked man, the stink of his anxious sweat in my face. He levered away from me with his waist and knees, still gripping the shotgun. I grabbed the double barreled over-under guns, twisted with all my strength, and kneed my opponent in the groin.

He lost wind, and I rolled up with the weapon, my boots grabbing ahold of a rocky patch in the slick snow. But I was halfway off balance. I flung the barrel of the gun around toward him, but started to teeter.

"Give it up, Ted," I said, the muzzle catching the rim of his glasses under the mask. Jerking the gun toward the stars, I exposed him even as I fell backwards, cradling the precious shotgun.

Staggering, Ted took three steps back and ducked as gunfire erupted behind me. Biff Barlow swept past on his palomino with six-gun action blazing as the kidnap wagon rolled away down the street.

I sat up in time to see one of Albert's kidnappers topple sideways over the rim of the wagon box and hit the ground. Heard Biff yell, "I got one!"

The wagon slid to a sideways stop as the driver jumped down to help the fallen man.

Wanting more than anything to encourage Biff along in his success, I had my hands full with Ted Roberts. Crouching in the middle of the street, a stout little gun had appeared in Ted's hand and flame spat from the muzzle.

I jerked to the side as the slug slapped ground in a shower of ice.

I appealed to our past partnership. "This ain't the way to treat your friends, Ted."

"We've never been friends," he hissed, and a second pop sent more lead my way. Without his glasses, he was half-blind. "You've never done squat but make fun of me. You and all your Pony Boy pals. Well, now your whole damn lot will get what they've always deserved."

"Starting with Albert?"

"Starting with Tony Pike." Another shot, this one thumping into the denim of my coat, ripping a corner from its padded fleece shoulder. I was letting him get too close.

"I suppose you took care of John Wade, too? Was it your bunch who took him out?"

"You forgot who you are, Gus. You signed an agreement to be part of the Association. If you're too squeamish to dispense justice," Ted said, "you can't be upset if somebody else takes care of your business."

"Where's John Wade?"

"You'll never find him in this lifetime." He was right over the top of me with Kid Wade's British Bulldog only inches from my face.

Point-blank, he couldn't miss.

Neither could I.

"I know damn well who I am."

Ted Roberts's expression showed nothing but physical shock as both fired barrels of my shotgun tore through his chest.

Vigilante, Pony Boy. John Augustus, or August John.

Or just Gus — spattered with blood on a winter street.

Ted fell over sideways, twitching, and I hauled myself upright. Cap Burnham was there on one side and the sheriff on the other, keeping me steady. "Holy Mary, Mother of God," Cap said over the pitiful remains of Ted Roberts. I handed over the shotgun, and Biff Barlow reined in.

"Did you stop them?" I asked. "What happened to the Kid?"

"Winged one of them, but he managed to

climb back aboard. I don't know where they were fixing to go, but they had an escape route planned."

"Son of a bitch," Hershiser said. "Never lost a man in custody before."

I followed the sheriff's gaze down the street.

Biff said, "It's the end of Albert for sure."

The next morning, Sheriff Hershiser took the train back to O'Neill by himself, and Cap Burnham went back to Carns, and right then neither of them had any idea what happened to Albert. Though at breakfast we predicted doom for him, we nodded politely at Biff when he said there was always the chance the men who stole him away might be his friends putting on a show for our benefit. "It would be just like Kid Wade to be twenty miles away right now, drinking a highball, laughing at us from afar."

In deference to Henry Richardson, Cap and the sheriff agreed Ted Roberts should be laid to rest as a member of the Association, noting to all that he gave his life in the line of duty, for the love of justice.

As warped as his sense of justice might have been.

Biff continued spinning his mad theories

290

while we prepared our horses for the trip to Pleasant Valley, and he was speculating on a possible location for Kid Wade's hideout "somewhere on Plum Creek again," when the report came in that they found a man hanging from a whistling post along the railroad tracks headed east into town, a half mile outside of Bassett.

Mrs. Martin called a local doc who acted as town coroner to identify the body.

I asked Biff to wait for the official word of Albert's demise.

While I rode straight for Virgil Manke's house.

CHAPTER TWENTY-FIVE

Ted Roberts, who'd never been much of anybody, had hurled an accusation at me. "You forgot who you are, Gus," meaning I wasn't the vigilante killer he expected me to be, but when I killed *him,* I wasn't a Pony Boy either.

Each of us are what we make of ourselves, and that bright, sunny morning they found Kid Wade dead alongside the tracks, I was busy as anything with my insides. Riding Ed along the Long Pine street down into the canyon road and around the long, tree-lined bend to Manke's spread, I was busy building an identity.

Measuring the needed sense of responsibility. Cutting the boards of vengeance. Framing up the retaining walls of my soul.

I meant to be home that night to Trudy, Sonny, and McGee the dog. With winter dark falling early, I didn't have a lot of time. What I did have was plenty of practice building things, and not just the barn at Pleasant Valley.

In the last few months I'd built new friendships. I'd built comradery and trust.

Enmity too.

Because no matter how it was spun for the newspapers, Henry Richardson was never going to be my pal. Not after I'd practically cut his nephew in two.

Especially not after my visit to Virgil Manke's place.

I rode up a winding trail, out of the canyon, and Manke's big white house on the hill came into view followed by the barn's rooster-topped weather vane — a black mark on a blue sky.

The layout had always given me a thrill. To see such splendor, laid out with order and precision, once made me feel all was right with the world.

Today I saw the flaws.

The despondent barn's snow-laden roof was hail-smacked and sagging, in need of repair. The pretentious house had a cracked window. A once-proud corral fence tilted sidewise, broken by a fallen spruce tree, unattended, left to crumble with dry, brown needles spackled with patches of frost and ice.

I hobbled Ed at the edge of the property

and snuck down along the back side of the corral fence to the rear of the barn. To the secret pens Albert told me about, underneath and inside.

My eyes took a few seconds to adjust to the murky dark. For just a second, I doubted.

Then a soft breath and an easy whinny turned my head.

"I'm here, girl. You remember me, don't you?"

There was no reason she should. Shady Jane had been away from her master for nearly three months, and I was just one of more than a dozen men who'd once watched her nearly outrun Miss Baghdad.

A sin for which she had been jailed.

She brushed my hand with her muzzle, and leaned into my scratching her chin.

I took a minute to build a smoke, relishing the taste of the tobacco in the clean, storm-swept air.

"You're lucky to be alive," I told the lovely bay mare. "But let's go ahead and get you out of here."

It took less than a minute to find a blanket and saddle amidst the fine leather tack. Another five to get her set up and led outside.

Before I rejoined her, I made sure there

were no additional horses in the barn. Then I just happened to toss my lit cigarette into the straw.

Accidents. They do have a way of happening.

The sun was high in the forenoon sky when I walked Shady Jane around to the front road where Manke's racetrack stretched across his open field beside the cottonwood trees and pines.

I was still enough of a Pony Boy to get in and out without anybody knowing it.

I wanted Virgil Manke to know it.

So I waited with a casual stance as he hobbled down the hill from his house.

Shady Jane's reins in one hand, my Peacemaker in the other.

"Hold on there, you," he said at a distance of more than ten yards. "Who are you to wander — Oh! John Augustus, it's you."

The recognition came an instant before he saw the gun.

Then his eyes beheld Shady Jane.

Manke waddled into place, his pompous parade of white hair bouncing along under a fat shellacking of bay rum salve.

"What's this all about, son?"

I waved the pistol at his right arm, hanging in a sling.

"You hurt yourself, did you?"

"Tripped and fell from my porch while feeding the cats."

"Is that so?"

"My God," he said, play-acting a part, "is that Frymire's horse? Son, did you locate Shady Jane, or . . . ?"

"Save it, Virgil. Before you all got going with your necktie party last night, Albert told me about your barn. He admitted taking Jane from Ben's place, delivering her here for you."

"Naturally, I have no idea what you're talking about. As a matter of fact, I think you might have stolen Jane yourself. You wouldn't be trying to pin something on me?"

"Albert says he got $100 for the delivery. I figured I'd give her back to Ben for free. I'm sure he'll be grateful to you for these three months boarding her. In fact, I'll send him down your way to settle the bill. Maybe Biff Barlow and I will join him."

"Hear now . . ."

"I figure we could use the same rope you boys used on Albert. It worked so good the first time."

Manke's face blanched and was the same color as his hair. "How dare you."

"Squawk all you want, Manke. It's just you and me, here."

"It's my word against yours."

I climbed on Shady Jane's back and nudged her forward, forcing Manke to take a step back. "Bullets don't care about words. Neither does a sturdy piece of hemp."

Manke ran his free hand through his hair, combing furrows in the reluctant, stiff field of locks. When he looked at me again, his frantic eyes were desperate.

"I'll admit it," he said. "I was trying to protect his name, but I may as well tell you. It was Ted Roberts who took Jane."

"That's not what Kid Wade said."

"You'd take the word of a lying horse thief over mine?"

"I'd take the word of my friend over a lying horse thief." Once strong Virgil Manke in his heavy wool coat was now reduced to a panic-ridden, stumbling bird with a bullet-torn wing. Looking down from Frymire's beautiful strong bay, I pitied him. "Now get out of my way before I shoot you for sport."

He quickly ducked aside and Shady Jane took three steps along the trail before I reined her in. Turning in the saddle, I caught the first whiffs of smoke, saw the plume of a swirling gray cloud erupt into the sky.

"Oh, by the way," I said, nodding to the

left, before I rode away, "looks like your barn's on fire."

Late in the summer, John Wade's body was found in a shallow grave, twenty miles from Bassett near Ash Creek. Death attributed to person or persons unknown.

And Albert Wade, laid to rest on Bassett Hill, wouldn't stay buried.

Even in death, I couldn't trust the Kid.

Just as predicted, he turned up again as a pile of prairie bones in the Bassett, Nebraska, Oddfellows Lodge, kept busy doing his penance as part of the member rituals.

Cap Burnham disbanded the Niobrara Mutual Protective Association and eventually made it to the Nebraska Legislature where he served an honorable number of years.

Ben Frymire's Shady Jane became a famous racetrack trotter, and Virgil Manke died penniless.

As for me, that year in Pleasant Valley, 1884, we lost Sonny, but gained a son, healthy and strong in Trudy's tender care.

I had always been ashamed to cry, but with both events I wept a long time.

And some nights, for more reasons than I care to discuss, I still sit under the stars and weep.

Having cast a wide loop, my friends and I cleared the Niobrara River valley of a ring of desperate cutthroats, but also most assuredly managed to snare ourselves.

AUTHOR'S NOTE

On December 4, 1883, the *Holt County Banner* reported to a gossip-hungry audience of Nebraska readers that Kid Wade, the infamous outlaw who'd been terrorizing the Niobrara River valley, had been shot dead on the banks of Plum Creek while attempting to steal a team of mules. The story had everything the immigrants of the rough country hoped for: Foster Richardson, a wronged man with good character, a known scoundrel caught in the act, a decisive end — even some high-minded moralizing from the editor.

The problem with the story is that is wasn't true.

The man Foster Richardson shot, if in fact there occurred such an incident, has been lost to history. But the story remains on the front page of the *Banner,* more than 140 years later. I never found a retraction, though further exploits of the Kid were breathlessly reported, including the story of his actual execution on February 6, 1884.

It wasn't the first time Kid Wade would rise from the grave.

By all accounts, a physically small, unattractive gent, Albert Wade rose in the vacuum created by Doc Middleton's absence to become, arguably perhaps, Nebraska's greatest horse thief and second best-known outlaw.

Stories of the Kid's life would continue to be told, lies handed down, exploits embroidered with bias and local color. In the 1930s, writers who were just kids in the 1880s looked back on those unorganized days and brought a renewed interest in history along the Running Water. T. Josephine Haugen shared her personal remembrance of Kid Wade in the January–March, 1933 issue of *Nebraska History* magazine. After his capture in Le Mars, Iowa, and while in the custody of vigilantes, his party stopped at the Haugens' family cabin where "the prisoner showed no concern. He sat playing with the doorknob and laughed freely as he answered the cross examination by Richardson."

Wade's lighthearted, kind demeanor is a constant in such tales. So much so, that along with his mentor, Middleton, he became one of the West's true antiheroes. Corrupt, certainly. Unscrupulous, maybe. A good guy to pass time with — absolutely. Taken to the extreme, he becomes a charming rogue in Will Henry Spindler's 1941 novel/memoir, *Rim of the Sandhills*. Big on melodrama, short on facts, Spindler wrote from memory and from the heart, spinning "A true picture of the old Holt County horse thief-vigilante days."

I'm beyond grateful to the Missouri River Regional Library and the state college at Chadron, Nebraska, for facilitating the interlibrary loan that placed Spindler's work in my hands, if only for a short time.

The legend would continue to grow, fertile ground for tourism along Nebraska's Outlaw Trail Scenic Byway, Highway 12 from Sioux City to Valentine. Inspiring books, songs, and even lending his likeness to a bottle of wine, Kid Wade lived.

Like Elvis, JFK, and other folk heroes after him, his physical remains became the topic of skeptical inquiry and conspiracy fodder. According to Judge Lewis Canenburg, in the eighth chapter of a serial piece published in the Bassett, Nebraska, newspaper, the body of Kid Wade was cut down from its railroad whistling post and laid on a pile of wood in front of a local merchant's store. Pieces of the hang rope were cut and sold to locals as keepsakes, and the Bassett constable, Fred Kramer, then moved the body to Canenburg's barn until he was buried on Bassett Hill. Only to be exhumed later as a complete skeleton and used, according to Haugen, for ceremonial purposes at the Bassett, Nebraska, Oddfellows Lodge.

The mix of legend, half truth, and historic fact surrounding Kid Wade that still persists is astounding. For every anecdote, there's a counter-story. For every fact in print, there's probably an exception published elsewhere. I have done my best in the fictionalized narrative to adhere to a framework of truth as revealed by the primary sources while necessarily reserving a storyteller's artistic license. It's been great fun, and wouldn't have been possible without standing on the shoulders of those men and women who were passionate about the Kid before me.

First and foremost thanks to the *Nebraska Historical Society* and Michelle Maltas at *Advantage Preservation* for the contribution of their DVD Newspaper Archive 1880–1884. With such a wonderful resource, articles from the *Stuart Ledger,* the *Knox County News,* and the *Holt County Banner* were infinitely easier to access.

Gratitude to the Holt County Historical

Society for their beautiful Centennial Edition book, *Before Today: A History of Holt County Nebraska,* lovingly penned by Western Writers of America Spur Award–winner Nellie Snyder Yost.

Acknowledgment also goes, in no particular order, to Will Henry Spindler, Josephine Haugen, Harold Hutton, Janet Eckmann, Curt Arens, and Danny Liska.

Kid Wade was hanged, and Cap Burnham declared victory of sorts in a letter to the public published in the February 6, 1884, edition of the *Holt County Banner.*

But vigilante activity in Nebraska was far from over.

Pushed west with the railroad, the frontier gave way to law and order, but not all at once, and not always in neat and tidy ways.

But that's a story for another day . . .

Richard Prosch
Somewhere south of the Running Water

ABOUT THE AUTHOR

Richard Prosch grew up planting corn, tending cattle, and riding the Nebraska range in a beat-up pickup and a '74 Camaro.

With his wife he developed licensing style guides for several cartoon properties and worked with Tribune Media Services and the Hallmark Channel. In the 2000s, Richard built a web development studio while winning awards for illustration and writing (including a Spur Award from the Western Writers of America). His work has appeared in novels, numerous anthologies, *True West, Wild West, Roundup,* and *Saddlebag Dispatches* magazines, and online at *Boys' Life.*

Richard lives on a Missouri acreage with his wife, Gina, son, Wyatt, and an odd assortment of barn cats.

The employees of Thorndike Press hope you have enjoyed this Large Print book. All our Thorndike, Wheeler, and Kennebec Large Print titles are designed for easy reading, and all our books are made to last. Other Thorndike Press Large Print books are available at your library, through selected bookstores, or directly from us.

For information about titles, please call:
  (800) 223-1244

or visit our website at:
  gale.com/thorndike

To share your comments, please write:
  Publisher
  Thorndike Press
  10 Water St., Suite 310
  Waterville, ME 04901

DATE DUE

PRINTED IN U.S.A.